TUNNELS and other short stories

ISBN-13:   978-1979582445

ISBN-10:   1979582440

Cover Design by Red Cape Graphic Design

www.redcapepublishing.com

For all the amazing horror writers I have connected
with recently, many of whom have given me such
great feedback on my work

ABOUT THE AUTHOR

This is the second collection of short horror stories from author Peter Blakey-Novis. Peter lives with his wife and four children in a small town in Sussex, England. As well as being a keen cook and wine enthusiast, Peter has been writing poetry and short stories for almost twenty years. An excitement for literature and storytelling has led to Peter now begin work on his third novel, as well as this range of short stories. Peter has also written children's stories, aimed specifically for his own children, currently close to being published.

KEEP UP TO DATE!

More information about the author can be found on his website as well as social media profiles listed below. You can also subscribe to the email mailing list via the website for exciting news about future releases, as well as accessing short stories direct to your mailbox! If you have any comments or would like to just get in touch feel free to email directly at the address below. Happy reading!

Twitter:
www.twitter.com/pjbn_author
Facebook:
www.facebook.com/pjbnauthor
Web:
www.redcapepublishing.com/our-authors
Email:
redcapepublishing@outlook.com

CONTENTS

21

A picture-perfect family; Mum, Dad, two boys and a really pretty girl. They had arrived yesterday. I watched them through the trees as they positioned that new-looking caravan into place, under the direction of the campsite owners. It was hot, and I was sweating under my camouflage. But I couldn't very well wear anything else and risk being seen. I returned today. I continued to watch, studying the way they interacted with each other. They all had smiles on their faces; not a care in the world. It was mid-afternoon; it wouldn't be dark for another five or six hours. I could wait. There was no way of knowing how long they would be staying for so it had to happen tonight, I couldn't risk coming back tomorrow only to find they had gone.

The site was perfect in so many ways. It was relaxed, especially from a security aspect. It was accessible on three sides to anyone willing to walk through the dense trees; the only vehicular access came from one long, unlit lane. There was no gated entry, nothing to stop the guests coming and going at any time that they chose. Such a stroke of luck that I found it; this will be much easier than last time. That place had turned into an absolute nightmare, and it could so easily have been my final time.

The build up, the routine, the planning. These were the parts that held the most excitement for me. The watching. It was like a military operation, and I was good at it. Even if the army didn't want me. That was their loss, their mistake. Maybe if they had taken me in, I wouldn't be doing this now. Perhaps that pretty family would have been able to enjoy their holiday without having it cut short. For an hour I stood among the trees, motionless, just my eyes moving around as I surveyed the other campers.

It was much less busy than the places I had been to previously. One side of the field, to the east of the entry point, it was filled with caravans, all nearly identical. They appeared to be the same size; four-berth most likely. I counted them up yesterday; eleven of them. Still all eleven there. I had walked by last night, a little after midnight, for a kind of reconnaissance mission; I wanted to see if anyone would notice me, but they didn't. They never do. None of the caravans looked as if they were up to traveling, and it was almost certain that they were left there all year round. Which meant there was a good chance that they were empty, or certainly most of them.

In the south-eastern corner, there were three tents, large ones. Could have been ten or twelve-man tents, all arranged with the entrances facing each other, surrounding a square of windbreakers. Within the windbreakers were chairs, cooking equipment, and so on. The residents, whom I assumed were one large group, had been the only ones still up when I took my wander last night. Seven adults, sitting around a fire drinking beer and cursing whilst their hoard of unruly offspring tried to get to sleep. Thankfully no dogs this time. I hate dogs.

The new family were as far from everyone as they could be, claiming a solo pitch on the western edge of the field. They must think they are too good to set up close to the others; and maybe they are right. Even so, that arrogance only serves to make my life so much easier. I struggled to pull myself away, absorbed in the game that the children were playing. I watched in amusement as the older boy and girl threw a ball to each other, to the annoyance of their younger brother who stood no chance in catching it. Eventually, he stopped trying, stomping away and calling for his mummy. I watched as the older boy, a tall, dark-haired creature with a wicked grin, shouted after his brother; "Stop being such a baby, you little loser!" The kid must have been four or five and, briefly, I felt a little pity for him. I stared at the older boy. *You'll be first*, I promised him. Only a few more hours to go; time to finish the preparations.

I returned a little after dusk, following the lane but staying just within the tree line in case any cars drove by. No-one came along the dark road; all remained silent until I reached the entrance to the site. This was the riskiest part; the twenty or thirty yards that ran alongside the toilets and showers were well lit and stayed that way all night. The coast looked clear, but there was no way of knowing if someone was about to come out of the toilets. I just needed to walk confidently, as if I belonged there. I felt my heart beat more quickly, the adrenalin flooding my system. I heard a toilet flush as I took a few hurried steps into the darkness, just beyond the reach of the lights. Seconds later, I was standing against the western edge, completely enveloped in darkness, as I watch an overweight female in a dressing gown make her way back towards the trio of tents in the far corner.

I looked towards my destination and saw four people sat around a fire, their faces illuminated by the flames. The youngest was missing, presumably already asleep inside the caravan. My right hand reached into the deep pocket of my cargo pants, caressing the switchblade that waited there. *Only for emergencies,* I reminded myself. I took sideways steps, hidden by the blackness, as I edged closer to them. The caravan was positioned almost up to the edge, with perhaps three or four feet between the rear of it and the start of the woodland. I took a step back, slipping into the pitch blackness, avoiding the light which shone from the caravan's window.

My plan hinged largely on one hope; that it would be a warm enough evening for them to leave a window open. If not, then I would need to force the door which, although not impossible, would increase the risks considerably. I was in luck, however, as I saw three of the windows still wide open. In the past, I had managed to get inside before the owners, hiding myself in the built-in closet of a larger caravan. When this one arrived, I considered repeating that plan as it had worked out well before. I searched on-line for the floor plan, located a suitable hiding place, and kept my fingers crossed. It would work, I knew that, but they were sat too near the door for me to be able to sneak in. Plan B was the windows, which relied on them not to close them before heading to bed. *It's a warm and sticky evening,* I thought. *It'll be fine, just wait it out.* Half an hour later, I watched as mum ushered the two siblings inside, the mean boy and the pretty girl, drawing the curtains. After another ten minutes of watching dad prodding at the fire with a stick, mum returned.

She made her way to her partner; a duvet wrapped around her despite the warmth of the evening. I watched from my position, alone in the dark, as she sat on his lap. I could make out a slight rhythm to their motion as they kissed, and I wondered if they were doing more beneath that duvet. I only watched, transfixed, certain that they must want to be seen if they are behaving like that in the open. I felt a brief wave of confusion as I looked upon them with both disgust and arousal, but their moment came to a sudden end with the call of a child. From the muffled sounds, I made out that the smallest child was awake, mum to the rescue as she headed inside. Dad, a tall, thin man in his early forties, gathered up the empty cans and tidied up a little before following her inside. It was almost time and the nerves began to set in, the twisting, knotted butterflies felt that they wanted to burst from my stomach.

Remaining still for fear of crunching a branch beneath my feet, I stood transfixed on the caravan, willing off the lights. There was no way to see in with the curtains closed. I checked my watch; almost eleven. The lights went out at eleven-twenty. The windows were left open. I took a step forward and paused. My eagerness may have almost led to disaster. *If they were doing what it looked like, and haven't finished, then they are probably carrying on now,* I pondered. *Give them a bit longer. Be patient.* I crept alongside the caravan, trying to listen for any sounds that would indicate anyone was awake. There was nothing; no television, no talking, no sex noises.

I took one last glance across the field; only the large group in the far corner showed any signs of life, but they would not be able to see me from there. I peered around the front to check the coupling and found the caravan to still be attached to the Range Rover. I slipped by backpack off and unzipped it, straightening out the tubing and feeding one end through the open window. There were so many things that could go wrong, and I did not like not knowing exactly where each of them was sleeping. Nevertheless, it had to be done. I fixed my end of the tube to the unit I had designed myself and switched it on. The battery whirred, seeming much louder in the silence of the field than it had previously. I positioned it beneath the caravan and scurried back under the cover of darkness among the trees. I waited. Ten minutes. Then another ten. There was no change, no sounds, no lights coming on. *Now or never!* I made my way to collect the equipment, placing it safely back inside my bag. The contents of the vapour were my own variation on a recipe in the Chemical Warfare Handbook, utilizing the effects of a veterinary tranquilizer that should have rendered the caravan's occupants unconscious by now. If the dose had been evenly taken in, I'd expect the larger people to come around in two to three hours. But that little boy would be a different matter; it could be eight hours. And that's if he even wakes up at all.

I attached my small, homemade gas mask to my face and managed to pop the catch on the door with the switchblade, closing it quietly behind me. They looked so peaceful; the three children on a pile of duvets across the main living space. I crept past them, opening the first of two doors on my right. A toilet. I carefully opened the second door and found the parents in bed, a duvet covering them up to their heads, appearing as if asleep. Satisfied that all was going to plan, I clicked on my torch and began to search for the keys. Not anywhere obvious in the living space. *Must be in his jeans. Bingo.* I found them lying among the clothes he had dumped on the floor before climbing into bed, slipped them into my pocket, and made my way outside. I locked the caravan, despite being almost certain that its occupants would not awaken during the journey. *Just in case,* I told myself. *Don't want anyone jumping out and making a scene.*

Sliding into the driver's seat, I turned the key, allowing the Rover's engine to purr. I couldn't see anyone else on the campsite but decided that there was enough open space for me to move around towards the entrance before switching on the lights. Once I had the car facing the lit-up area around the facilities, I flicked on the headlights, and we were on our way. I had at least two hours until anyone began to stir and, to be on the safe side, I had selected a destination only an hour away. I was confident that it was far enough from the original extraction point and would also afford me ample time to get my guests into position. The campsite would not necessarily raise any concerns over guests leaving earlier than planned; after all, they had paid upfront on arrival so no loss to the owners. Chances are there would be a few days before anyone reported them missing and by then, I would be long gone.

Fifty-minutes later, I turned the Range Rover on to a chalky, quarry path. The location was isolated; dark and silent. The structures surrounding the path were parts of a disused steel works; great, red clunks of metal protruding from the ground, rising all around me. I dragged the caravan along until I was out of sight of the road, parking it up next to the steel barn which had acted as a makeshift staff room long ago. Yanking open the door with a clang of metal, the sound echoing around me, I went inside to grab supplies. One bag of cable ties and a dirty sheet, which I cut into five long strips.   We were far enough from anyone that screams for help would go unanswered, but I did not want to have to listen to five people yelling at me. It made me anxious, and when I get anxious I can become disorganized and confused. But there was no confusion as to why I was there at that moment for I knew, beyond any doubt, that it was the only way that I could be taken seriously. The only way that those bastards who dismissed me as a freak, as not good enough, as an idiot - that they would know my name.

Cautiously, I unlocked the caravan and opened the door, slowly. Still no sign of movement. I began with the adults as they posed the most threat to me, removing the duvet and binding their hands and feet with cable ties, wrapping the dirty cloth around their mouths.   Still they did not stir.   I looked down at them on the bed, both fully nude, bound and helpless. My thoughts sank into the gutter for a moment as I looked at her; she would never know. *No!* I told myself. *That's not who you are. That's not what you want to be remembered as.* I repeated the process with the three children, all of whom were clothed in pyjamas, and stood outside to wait. Thirty-six minutes passed before I heard a thud.

Re-entering the caravan, I saw the three children still out for the count. It was the adults that had come around first, just as I had expected; their larger masses would have recovered from the toxin more quickly than their children could. I cocked my head to the side as I gazed down at him, naked and restrained, trying pathetically to drag himself along the floor. He couldn't lift his head high enough to see me properly, so he rolled himself over, the gag muffling whatever obscenities he was attempting to throw in my direction. I allowed myself a little laugh.

"If only you could see how ridiculous you look!" I told him, enjoying my position of power. "Helpless on the floor, flapping that tiny thing about." I glanced at his manhood. "Are you cold?" He writhed about on the floor in anger, his eyes wide as he assessed his situation. "Is that pretty lady awake yet?" I asked. This seemed to refuel his anger, his protectiveness becoming even more evident. "Oh don't worry. It's not like that. I'm not that kind of monster." I stepped over him to check the bedroom and found her in the fetal position, sobbing as best she could with the rag in her mouth.

"Don't worry, honey," I told her. "It'll be over soon enough. I need you two to come with me; I know it'll be difficult to walk in your situation, but I'll help you up and you'll need to try. OK?" She just continued to sob, making no attempt to get off of the bed or even look at me. *Rude,* I thought, approaching the man.

"Looks like you're up first then," I told him, putting my hand under his armpits and dragging him towards the door. He wouldn't stay still, which I guess is understandable, but it made the process difficult for me. I don't cope with stress very well; it makes me itchy. Once I had his head poking out of the door, facing down at the three small steps, I moved behind him for the last push. He landed in a heap in the dust, groaning loudly as his shoulder made a popping sound. "Dislocated, most likely," I told him. Still he kept trying to talk to me, perhaps to beg and plead, perhaps to threaten me. Whatever message he wanted to convey was in vain, I had made the mistake of talking to them before, and it only muddled me up. *They're the enemy, they will say anything to stop you carrying on with your work, they would kill you if they could,* I reminded myself. I locked the caravan and dragged him into the barn, under the glow of electric lights that I had fixed up on the previous day. He scouted around the room, clocking the chairs. Five chairs.

It was difficult, but I hauled him onto one of the chairs, wrapping ten feet of thick, electrical cable around him for extra security. Now, even if he tried to stand, he would be taking the chair with him. "I need you to stay here," I told him, leaning forward a little so out eyes could meet. "Do you understand?" He nodded, panic across his face. "If you move, I'll kill someone." Again, he nodded.

The children still did not stir, so I picked up the smallest. He was light enough for me to carry out without any problem. Only he didn't feel right; paler than I expected. *Shit!* The gas *was* too much for his mass; I suspected it may be. *He's going to go berserk when he finds out!* I told myself, knowing that I needed to get everyone restrained in the barn at the same time. I decided to put the little child on the chair furthest from his father, in the hope that he would think he was still only unconscious. I strapped him in under his father's glare, but this time he did not try to speak to me.

The other two kids weren't an issue; both light enough to carry, both only beginning to stir. Four out of five in place. Ten minutes, maximum, I had spent between grabbing the last child and returning to the caravan. In the space of those ten minutes, she had gone from helplessly restrained on the bed to having disappeared. There weren't any hiding places inside, she was not in the toilet, and she surely could not have walked far. I glanced around in a panic - the utensil drawer was open. *Could she have dragged herself to the drawer and found something to cut the ties with? It wouldn't be easy but not impossible. Shit! Stupid me for thinking she was being complicit, just lying there.*

"I have your whole family in here," I yelled from the barn door. "I suggest you get here now, or I'm going to start taking bits off of them." Nothing. I scanned around with my torch, but she could be anywhere. *Fuck!*

"Right," I told the man. "I'm going to take your gag off. I want you to call her back here, right now! If she doesn't come back quickly, then I kill him." I pointed my switchblade at the body of the youngest child. His father's eyes widened, nodding quickly.

"Helen!" he yelled. "You have to come back. Please. He's going to kill Harry!" As he shouted these words, I heard muffled screams coming from behind me, the older children having woken up into this nightmare. I flashed my torch out of the barn door, revealing nothing of Helen's whereabouts.

"I warned you!" I hissed, before standing behind little Harry and jabbing my blade through his neck. A steady stream of red sprayed from his jugular as tears fell from my prisoners. They did not need to know he was already dead; not that it would have made their loss any more bearable. I stepped behind that taller boy, the one who had been horrible to Harry earlier that day. Looking to his father, I repeated my threat. "Get her back here. Now!" Helen's disappearance spoiled things for me; I felt rushed in case she managed to get help. This is not how it was meant to be and, if I couldn't find her, then I would be one person short of target. Someone else's blood would be on her hands.

Four times he called to Helen, all to no avail. I stood, once again, at the entrance to the barn with a torch in one-hand and a blood-stained blade in the other.

"Helen!" I called. "I'm counting to ten. Then you're lanky shit of a son is dead." I paused, listening intently into the darkness. Still nothing. "Then I'll count to ten again, before slitting your daughter's throat. You'd better hurry up."

"Please don't," the man begged.

"It's hardly my fault!" I told him. "You married a right selfish bitch! She could have done what she was told, and little Harry would still be alive. Admittedly, not for very long, but she did cut his life a bit short." He did not know how to reply to me, staring instead, anger flickering in his eyes. I shouted towards the door. "Ten, nine.." I counted down, slowing a little as I approached the final number. Still nothing. *She's gone. Somehow.* It wasn't how I'd planned it, but the end result would be the same. Doing my best to appear in control, I walked up to that gangly youth and ended him with five rapid jabs of the switchblade to his chest. His eyes widened for a brief moment as blood gurgled from his mouth, and then nothing. Another life extinguished in a moment.

I turned to see his father attempt to run at me, ankles bound, a chair on his back, but he did not get far. I resisted using the knife on him, merely shoving him backwards with a crash of wood and a yelp from his already damaged shoulder. His daughter cried incessantly, but the gag stifled the sound enough for it not to bother me too much. I looked at her, staring a while until she turned her gaze from the floor to meet mine. She knew she would be next as well as I did, but the look of fear had changed to a look of acceptance, of sadness about something that she could not change. I felt something when our eyes met, something that I was not used to. *Remorse? Guilt?* I knew I was a monster; I never denied that. But I had an agenda, a target to reach. And it was not as if I did not value human life, or even that I enjoyed the killing. It was the hunt that I enjoyed, that I was good at. But I could not very well go to all the effort of extracting people and then letting them go afterward? I'd have been caught years ago if I did that!

Helen's apparent escape had presented a problem for me, and this was something I had not prepared for. It had never happened before, but perhaps I had become greedy. Or just wanted it to be over. The highest number of kills, confirmed kills that is, by any British serial killer is twenty. Some lady from long ago with a penchant for poison. Of course, that crazy doctor confessed to killing over two hundred a few years back, but it hasn't been proved. So I want twenty-one. That would make *me* the most prolific serial killer this country has ever seen. As I gazed at the girl, trying to identify what I was feeling at that moment, I thought back to the girl a few months ago; number 16. It was planned down to the last detail; her morning jogging route, the most secluded spots along it, the ideal method. I saw it as an assassination, a necessary target. I could not put my finger on it, but there was something about her that made her stand out. It could have been an air of superiority, a woman well beyond my reach, an annoyance she evoked simply by jogging past me that first time. The hit had been easy. I'd lunged at her as she passed some beach huts along a promenade, pulling her between two of them and slitting her throat. Then I was gone. Number 16. I just needed five more, and I could relax; it wouldn't matter if I got away with it for any longer. If Helen doesn't return, then I'm still one short and that won't do.

"One, two..." I began, loudly towards the door. "Nine, ten." Nothing. ""She really doesn't care about you lot, does she!" I declared, incredulous that a mother could run from her family in this way. "Well, she can't have gotten far," I stated, with a sigh. "You know I can't let you go," I told him, as he continued to grunt from his place on the floor. "But it would be monstrous of me to make you watch another of your children die. I'll give you this small mercy." I leaned down towards him, the reddened blade pointing at his neck. He fell silent, just staring into me in defiance. His gaze was fixed, even in death. The loss of life happened too quickly for his eyes to close, as my blade entered the side of his head, piercing through his left ear. The entire five inches went in, destroying his brain in a fraction of a second, gloopy grey and red lumps sticking to the knife as I retrieved it. He slumped to the floor, a dark pool forming around the wound. His daughter now having fallen silent; she knew what was coming.

I sat on the floor, talking to the girl for some time after killing her father. Not about anything especially meaningful, and the conversation was entirely one-sided, but it passed some time while I deliberated my options. What I needed to do was kill the girl and then find Helen. But in keeping the child alive for a while longer, perhaps it would draw Helen back once she realized that she could not get far. Only she *had* got far, much farther than I had expected anyway. If she had waited to return with the police, then my time would have been up; of that I have no doubt. And I would have been named Britain's second most prolific serial killer, meaning that nineteen people had died for nothing. However, she did not return with the police. My one-sided conversation was cut short by the sound of tyres on gravel outside the barn; the space illuminated by headlights. I jumped from my seated position and waited to the side of the open door, knife at the ready, listening as car doors opened and closed.

"Jesus Christ!" I heard an older-sounding man exclaim. "We should have waited for the police!"

"I couldn't," came Helen's distraught voice. I saw the outline of her figure take a step inside the barn, surveying the blood-soaked bodies of her husband and two of her children. She looked as though she would collapse, but she spotted her daughter still alive, and ran to try to free her. The police were on their way, and I knew there was little time. I stayed motionless for a moment, and this must have given the Good Samaritan the idea that the coast was clear. He edged his way into the barn, and I struck; quick, repeated jabs with the blade until he dropped to the floor. Helen frantically pulled at the cable ties that bound her daughter, but she could not free her. So I did.

"I only need one more," I told them. I looked at the girl and told her to run. To this day, I'm not sure why I had the sudden change of heart; maybe I wanted to leave a witness to describe the cold-blooded nature of my actions, maybe I grew a morsel of conscience. She looked to her mother, as if needing permission. Helen nodded sadly, and the girl was gone. I stared into Helen's eyes as I raised my blade, her face suddenly illuminated in the reflection of blue and red lights now coming from outside. My time was almost up, but I reached my goal with a swift slash of the throat; the warm, sticky spray coating my face before I dropped to my knees and placed my hands on my head. My work was complete, and now came the prize - the fame, the respect, and the notoriety.

The Box

Almost twenty years after he had finally been brave enough to start up his own business, Jack was finally bringing in enough money for his wife, Lisa, to not have to work. The majority came from carrying out house clearances, but he was also earning a noticeable amount on the side, selling on the items that he cleared which he deemed too good for the tip. Largely selling online, and studying countless antique and collectible guide books, he made a tidy profit selling everything from ornaments to toys, vintage clothing to antique furniture. The guide books were a huge help, pointing him in the right direction as to whether the items were worth selling at all and if so, how much he could hope to get for them. In his collection, it was almost guaranteed that anything of value would be listed there somewhere, which is why Jack was so puzzled that he could not find anything resembling the item in his hand.

"What do you think this is?" he asked Lisa, as he made his way to the kitchen. She said nothing, only turning to look at what he held in his hand. As he passed it to her, she studied the intricate patterns carved into all six faces of the cube, running her fingers across the smoothness of the black marble.   Each side looked to be around six inches, the pattern only being disturbed by a groove running all the way around, an inch below, presumably, the top.   On one face, there appeared to be a tiny keyhole, indicating that the box could be opened.

"Do you have the key?" Lisa asked, gently shaking the box. "It doesn't sound like there's anything in it."

"No key that I could see.   There weren't any boxes of junk, just large items really.   And I can't find this in any of the books, but it's too nice to throw out."

"God, don't throw it away!   It's really pretty," Lisa said, still transfixed by the patterns which had been so meticulously etched into the marble.

"As long as you're sure?" Jack asked. "You said I'm not allowed to keep any more junk in the house!"

"There's something different about this, we should keep it if you don't think it's worth much."

"Well, if it is, then it isn't listed in any of the books.   But I'll have a look online later and see if I can find anything similar." With all searches failing to provide any information, the box found itself placed on the mantelpiece alongside a host of other ornamental items which Lisa had given him permission to hold on to.   And there it remained, for almost a fortnight.

When Jack had begun his business, his oldest child, Steven, was eight. He was now twenty-seven, with a child of his own; four-year-old Maisie. Jack's grand-daughter was a whirlwind; at least, that was how they all affectionately referred to her. One Sunday each month the Jack and Lisa would cook a meal for their son, his wife, and Maisie, and every time something would get broken by the four-year-old bull in a china shop. It was never malicious; she was just clumsy, and her parents would apologize profusely each time. Usually, it was picture frames getting knocked from the wall, or glasses knocked from the table during dinner. On this occasion, Maisie's parents made an error of judgment, allowing her to bring a plastic toy with her; one that launched discs at a potentially lethal velocity.

It was as the four adults were chatting in the kitchen, watching pans bubbling away on the hob, that they heard the little shriek. It was a familiar sound, the same noise that Maisie had emitted whenever she had broken something that did not belong to her. As everyone turned to look in the direction of the sound, Steven let out a sigh.

"You may have to start child proofing the house!" he declared. Lisa did not take the comment as a joke.

"Maybe you shouldn't have allowed her to bring a weapon with her!" she stated. "I really think that you need to get her seen; it isn't normal to be breaking stuff all the time."

"She's just being a child," Jack said. "I'm sure it's fine." Steven made his way towards the living room and stopped in his tracks. His daughter was kneeling on the wooden floor, with her back to him, making a heaving sound, as though she were choking on a hair ball.

"Maisie?" he asked. Slowly, she turned towards her father; her hands scrunched tightly into fists. As his gaze moved from her hands to her face, Steven's eyes widened as he saw that the skin around her face was covered in some kind of black powder. The heaving sound stopped as she looked at him, smiling widely, her teeth blackened by whatever substance was on her face.

"Dad!" Steven called, the hint of panic being apparent. Jack made his way into the living room.

"What's happened?" he asked, staring at Maisie. "Shit, she's bleeding," Jack pointed out, noticing the deep red trickles emanating from his closed fists. Steven approached his daughter, taking her hands.

"Open your hands, honey," he said, as calmly as he could manage. By this point, the two women were stood in the doorway, trying to assess the situation before making any suggestions. Maisie continued to grin at her father, looking him in the eye, as she unclenched her fists. As her fingers unfurled, she displayed the fragments of marble, having changed from white to red with the blood. "What is that?" Steven asked, turning to his father.

"Some marble box I found at work. Don't know what it is; it was pretty so we kept it on the mantelpiece. Honey," Jack said, turning to his granddaughter. "Did you knock it off with your toy?" Maisie did not speak, simply continuing to grin at her father. "You should have just told us. You didn't need to pick it up; come to the bathroom and we'll have a look at your hands." The words seemed to register with the child, despite her silence, and she stood up, hands outstretched, palms upwards.

Lisa led her granddaughter to the bathroom, sending Maisie's mother to fetch the first aid box from a cupboard in the kitchen, while the men cleared up the remaining fragments of the marble box. Positioning the child on the lid of the toilet, Lisa examined her hands. There appeared to be a lot of blood, but once she had used tweezers to remove any fragments that were visible, and wiped over cuts, they did not appear anywhere near as bad, and it was a relief to see that medical treatment would not be required. Following the application of a few plasters, Lisa went on to use a wet wipe to clean Maisie's face. The black substance did not come off easily, leaving streaks of powder, and took some time to remove. Inside of the child's mouth was the most difficult as no-one wanted her to ingest it, so Lisa cleaned as well as she could manage with a damp flannel and ordered Maisie to brush her teeth. By the time the clean-up was deemed to be good enough, their dinner was ready. Through all of this, Maisie had still not uttered a word.

"I think we should get her to a doctor," Steven said, as the group took their places around the table. "We've got no idea what that black stuff was."

"It's Sunday," his wife reminded him. "It'll mean a trip to the hospital."

"I know, but she's not spoken since it happened. Something isn't right." The adults looked towards Maisie, still grinning at her father, not even seeming to have noticed the meal placed before her. "Eat up, before it gets cold," he told her, and they began to work through the roast lamb in silence, each of them glancing at the child who continued to stare, unmoving. By the time that the adults had finished their meals, Maisie had not taken a bite.

"You have to eat something," Lisa told her, stabbing a fork into a piece of meat. "Would you like some help?" Maisie's gaze was unflinching, still focused on her father, but she opened her mouth as if to accept being fed by her grandmother. Lisa took the cue and guided the food into Maisie's mouth, placing the fork back beside the plate. The child began to chew slowly and, suddenly, spat the meat from her mouth.

"Maisie!" he mother gasped.

"It's burnt, mother!" Maisie shouted.

"It most certainly is not," Lisa exclaimed, surprised by the girl's sudden rudeness. "It's a little on the rare side, if anything." Maisie's gaze switched quickly to her grandmother and before anyone could realize what was happening, Lisa felt the jab of the fork in her arm. She looked down and let out a little scream at the sight of all three prongs embedded in her skin. As she looked at Maisie's face, the girl grinned, twisting the fork ninety degrees, opening up the wound. Lisa jumped up from the table, backing away from the child, her good hand clutching her bleeding arm. As soon as the other adults had registered the violent act, they stood quickly, rushing to Lisa's aid. All except Steven, who grabbed his daughter and carried her upstairs.

"What have you done?" he begged, tears forming in his eyes.

"Stupid bitch shouldn't have burned the lamb," Maisie said in a matter-of-fact tone. "Don't be angry Daddy." Steven just stared at his daughter in disbelief.

"I'm sorry Maisie, but I am angry. You have been really naughty. You need to go and see if grandma is OK, and apologize."

"Who's Maisie?" the girl enquired, as genuinely as if she was asking any other question to which she expected an answer.

"Don't be silly, I'm not in the mood. You're Maisie."

"I'm Dot." With that, Steven stood up to check on his mother whom he could hear crying from the kitchen. "Don't go, I don't want you to leave me."

"I'm not leaving you; I'm only going to the kitchen. You stay here, please."

"Can I have a kiss before you go?" Maisie asked, sweetly. Steven bent down to kiss his daughter on the cheek, but she turned her head, catching him off-guard, and spitting into his face.

As he entered the kitchen, Jack was dressing Lisa's wound and neither of Steven's parents saw him approach. They only turned as they heard their daughter-in-law let out a gasp.

"What's that over your face?" she asked, staring at her husbands blackened grin. He did not reply. "Steven!" she stated.

"Who's Steven?" he asked, cocking his head to one side. "I'm William." His wife's face displayed a look of panic, of not understanding what was going on. "Would you like some gravy?" Steven asked his wife.

She did not answer, not following the question, so he decided for her. Grabbing the porcelain gravy boat from the table, Steven swung it into the side of his wife's head, knocking her to the floor, ceramic shard landing around her. Jack lunged towards his son, reacting to the situation with little thought. As he shoved Steven backwards, Jack felt a sharp burn in his side as he slumped onto the kitchen floor. His eyes were wide with terror as he gazed up at his four-year-old granddaughter, a bloodied carving knife her hands.

"Maisie," he whispered, trembling in shock.

"I'm Dot." Lisa did not stand a chance, fear having frozen her to the spot. She stood at the end of the kitchen, screaming at full volume, as she surveyed the carnage in front of her. She watched as her son knelt down, snapping the neck of his own wife, and felt as though she may pass out. Lisa did not have the opportunity to pass out, or any way of escaping the pain that followed. Her reactions were too slow to hold back the onslaught from the child, whose wild stabs sent Lisa to the floor, soaking the tiles in a deep crimson.

"We should go home now, Dot," Steven told his daughter, and the pair took each other's hands before making their way out onto the street.

"It all looks so different," Maisie said. "Do you know which way to go?"

"We'll find our way home," Steven assured her, and they began to wander in the direction that felt right, the route which would take them back to their recently cleared home, the one they had both died in, the one that had stored their ashes together in a beautiful marble urn.

Retribution

On the night that it happened, revenge was the only thing on my mind. Well, that and anger, shock, despair, and grief. But revenge dominated my thoughts. We were only married a year; not quite a whole year, in fact. It was six days before our first wedding anniversary that I found the front door ajar, a gap of no more than an inch, but enough to stand out as unusual. I was late home and, as much as I was in no way directly responsible for her death, the guilt weighed heavily upon me from that day on. I could have gone straight home from work like I always did. I could have told those people that I worked with, the people I don't even really like, that I would pass on going for a drink. It's my birthday! Melissa said, as excited as a child. Everyone is coming.

It wasn't true; not everyone was there. In our small office, there were twelve employees that day; seven of us walked into the pub. I wish it was six. I was driving, so used that as my excuse to leave after two pints. It was more than I should have had, and was out of character for me but, even at the age of thirty-one, peer pressure still got to me. I told Liz what I was doing. We always knew where the other one was, although I said it was someone from the offices' birthday, rather than naming Melissa. They had never met, and I had no sinister intentions, but I said it anyway.

As I pushed open the door, I called out her name. No reply. My heart beat increased involuntarily; I don't remember panicking at that point, simply unsure of the situation. My body knew that something was off. I poked my head into each of the downstairs rooms, finding no sign of Liz, no sign of a struggle. I dropped my briefcase in the hallway outside the living room. Still wearing my brogues, I ran up the newly carpeted stairs, making almost no sound. This fact struck me only later; she would not have heard him coming.

The door to our bedroom was closed, and my hands felt clammy as I turned the bronze knob. The door creaked as it opened, something that used to irritate me every night. This time it only added to the dread that was building up inside me. Then I saw her. I took a step forward, my eyes wide, my jaw slack. The crisp white bedding now soaked red, the side of her torso gaping open. I stared in silence, my brain trying to process the image before me. My beautiful wife, face down, fully nude. Dead. I did not dare to touch her, or anything else in the room, until the police arrived. I had seen enough crime series' to know that I would be the prime suspect.

The rest of that evening is a blur. The house was illuminated by flashing red and blue lights from outside; I was sat in the kitchen answering questions. I don't remember the police asking if they should contact anyone, but they must have. I remember my best friend Darren rushing into the house and hugging me. I don't know how long the police were there, but it must have been a few hours by the time the coroner had removed Liz from my life. It was only when they had all left, just Darren and I in the house, that I finally managed to cry. At that point, I did not know any details of Liz's last moments, but her nudity suggested the obvious.

Darren cleaned the room up for me, that much I remember. I couldn't face it and he just marched in there with some bin bags and stripped the bed, wiped down the sides which were still coated in dust from the forensics' guys, and tried his best to make it presentable. The mattress will have to go, he told me, offering to deal with that himself. He was trying to be practical, I suppose. I didn't hear from the police for almost a week, and I had been too timid to chase them up myself. If there was news, they would call, I thought. Then they did call.

They had arrested Steven Hayes. He was a junkie, with a string of previous convictions for burglary and assault. The police took me to a room at the station to talk, showing a mugshot of the man they had arrested. Seeing his face made it worse, only serving to enhance the images I had of him raping my wife. I asked if they were sure he was the one; I wanted to know what evidence they had found. One of your neighbours spotted someone matching his description acting suspiciously near your house that night, I was told. He had a knife on him, which matched the lacerations to your wife's body. He has a string of priors. He has no alibi. It all sounded pretty circumstantial to me, but the detective in command seemed convinced they had the right guy. It would go to trial that week. They would push for the death penalty, giving me the opportunity to apply for 'retribution'.

Capital punishment was only brought back in three years ago, largely to ease the financial burden of having to keep these monsters locked up for such long periods of time. It went to a public vote, narrowly passing. I voted against it; the death penalty always seemed barbaric to me. Now I wasn't so sure. Steven Hayes went to trial and, largely due to his history of serious offences, was found guilty by all twelve members of the jury. The hearing lasted less than a day, and I sat, stone-faced, listening to the prosecution detail how the accused had held Liz down and cut her open. Her time of death had been only one to two hours before I had called it in; I had been laughing in the pub while my wife bled to death. The jurors tutted and shook their heads when they heard that, although no semen had been found, the victim showed signs of having been penetrated with something. There was bruising around her thighs, and she had torn inside. There was no way to tell if this happened before, or after she was killed. The judge handed down the death penalty; the accused said nothing during the entire hearing except to plead 'not guilty'.

"What now?" Darren whispered to me as I watched them escort Hayes out of the court room. I looked at him blankly. "Let them do it or apply for retribution?" I would be lying if I said I hadn't thought about it, after all, revenge is a primal instinct, and I certainly wanted him to suffer. But doing it myself? I couldn't picture it in reality.

"I don't know if I can," I said, feeling guilty for what I saw as my weakness.

"Only you can make that choice, mate," Darren replied. "If it was me, I'd want to do the deed myself. You know they'll only give him the needle, and he'll drift off to sleep. No pain, no suffering. Just think about what Liz went through."

"You think I haven't been? I think about it every fucking day!" I hissed. "I just don't know if killing him myself will make me feel better."

"It will," Darren told me, looking me dead in the eye. "I'll do it. If you want, I mean. We can go together and just tell me what to do to him." I knew he was serious, trying to help in a rather messed up way, so I told him I would think it over. It only took half a bottle of whiskey for me to decide. I couldn't see any way that I could feel worse at that moment, and I was certain that the guilt from killing Hayes would be nothing compared to the guilt I felt over Liz's death.

Retribution was a curious idea really, something the left wing (myself included) found abhorrent and morally inexcusable. Capital punishment was one thing, but allowing relatives of victims to carry out the killing themselves seemed beyond wrong. But then the arguments for it became stronger with research. The society of psychiatrists and numerous mental health practitioners starting displaying the benefits; how it could help with the grieving process, provide closure, relieve guilt. I could not foresee an end to the grief, and a large part of me did not want to stop grieving, but the guilt was the most unbearable. If I could feel as if I had avenged her death, then perhaps the guilt would become more manageable. And, as Darren pointed out repeatedly, he is going to die anyway.

"What if we fail?" I asked, beginning to slur from the alcohol. "Remember that guy that got killed?" I was referring to a case from the previous year, in which a man called Tom something had been granted retribution rights to kill the drink driver who had run over his toddler. The tables had turned and before the authorities could get into the room, Tom had his neck broken by the prisoner.

"That guy was an idiot," Darren said. "He untied the fucking guy. All we have to do is go in there and stab him. He'll be restrained; it's not a bloody gladiator fight." I was nervous, anxious. Darren seemed too confident, but I put this down to him being supportive rather than relishing the idea of killing another human being. I filled out the forms and had them sent back via email while I was still drunk enough to think it was a good idea.

Three days was all it took before we were being led into the holding ward, my palms sweaty, heart racing. I felt sick, the combination of nerves and uncertainty in what I was about to do starting to take over. I almost backed out, but I had put both myself and Darren on the form, and if I didn't go in, then he would probably go ahead without me, adding to my guilt instead of relieving it.

"The prisoner is restrained," we were told by a bored looking warden. He was a big guy, late forties probably, who appeared numb to the horrors of his job. "Under no circumstances are you to remove his restraints. There is a table to the side with some implements that you can use. We will have guards posted outside the room at all times, and we will be watching on these monitors." He nodded towards a trio of screens in front of him. On the screens, I saw Steven Hayes from three different angles, tied to a hospital bed, with two guards in the room awaiting our arrival. "You have fifteen minutes, so please don't drag it out." I wondered then if the cleaning up fell on to the guards, and whether this is why they seemed as if everything was a huge hassle for them.

The door opened with a loud buzz as the warden pressed a button under his desk. The two officers inside the room gave us a curt nod as they left, presumably to watch on the screens outside. Darren eyed the silver trolley with an inappropriate grin.

"This looks pretty savage," he declared, holding up a shiny meat cleaver. "You want to go first?" I turned to look at Hayes. He looked as if he had accepted his fate, staring at the ceiling through watery brown eyes.

"I don't think I can," I muttered, the nausea growing inside me.

"What are friends for?" Darren asked and before I could respond, he marched over to the side of the bed and slammed the cleaver into the man's shoulder. There was a scream as it went in deep, a spray of blood hitting Darren in the face. He looked crazed as he brought the cleaver down again on the shoulder, and again, until Steven's entire right arm hit the floor with a thud.

"Do you want to say anything to him?" Darren asked me. "If so, better do it soon. He looks like he might pass out." I approached the bed, slightly afraid, mostly angry. This was my primal moment, my chance for vengeance.

"Why did you do it?" was all I could ask. It was what I wanted to know above all else. "Was it meant to just be a burglary?" I could feel my eyes welling up, but I fought the tears back.

"I didn't," he said, facing me. "I didn't." For a second, there was a flicker of doubt in my mind as I looked at him. A moment that was interrupted by Darren bringing the cleaver down on his chest in a frenzy, crunching through ribs until bloody bubbles came through from his hacked-up lungs. I heard a final gush of air escape Steven Hayes' body as the life drained out of him, leaving a crimson mess staring at the ceiling once more. Then the sickness came. I bolted out of the room to find somewhere to vomit, greeted by the guards who simply pointed to a door to indicate the toilets.

Darren came out a few minutes later. What I didn't know was that he had seized the moment when I left the room and the guards were briefly distracted, stealthily pulling his own knife from inside his workman's boots and slicing Hayes open along one side of his torso. On his way to putting the now-red cleaver back on the trolley, he casually carved a second notch in the knife's handle and hid it away.

One anonymous tip-off, he thought, giving one last glance at Hayes. That was all it took, and they were screaming for your blood.

Scratches

"What on earth are they doing now?" Angela asked me, becoming irritated that she could not get to sleep yet again. The new neighbours weren't especially noisy, but our bedrooms were only separated by one, seemingly thin, wall. In the month or so since they had moved in, we had heard all kinds of things and learned a lot about their routine from our position in bed, trying to get to sleep. One of them runs a bath at 10.45pm each day. There is often the muffled sound of conversation, which sometimes escalates to an argument. Once we could hear them having sex. *Only once, in almost five weeks,* I thought. *No wonder they don't sound happy.* The sound that was causing this evening's irritation was not talking, not shouting, and not even the groan of pipes as the bath water started to flow. It was scratching; a cross between the noise that one makes when stripping wallpaper with a scraper, and someone dragging fingernails across a rough surface.

"It's probably just mice," I said, immediately regretting it. Angela hates mice. She hates rodents of any kind, in fact, particularly if they are keeping her from sleeping.

"Then call pest control in the morning," she said, wedging her head in between her two pillows. I turned on to my side, my back facing Angela, and listened to the sound as it penetrated the darkness of our bedroom. *Scratch, scratch, scratch.* It was too quick to be the neighbour carrying out some home improvements; more like a scurrying sound. Like mice. I'd never had to use the pest-control people before, and money was tight, so I needed to be certain it was actually a problem. *Tomorrow I'll go next door and ask if they heard anything,* I decided, drifting off to the sound of unwelcome visitors in the skirting boards.

We overslept the following morning, rushing around to get out of the house on time and making no mention of Angela's pest-control demands. I didn't forget; I simply chose to put it off. It was too early in the morning to be knocking on doors, so I decided to wait until after work before speaking to our neighbours. *Or perhaps we should wait and see if we hear the sounds again tonight?* I was happy to ignore it, but knew that Angela would become more and more irritated if I did not do something to fix the problem. Of course, any problems like this fell to me to deal with, being the man of the house. As much as Angela proclaimed to believe in equal rights regardless of gender, what she actually expected was that her man should do as she commanded; being needed was something that I usually enjoyed, despite there being times when it became a bit much.

I arrived home at my usual time, which provided me with one peaceful hour before Angela was due home. I took this opportunity to search online for prices for pest control, discovering that an initial visit and treatment program was way beyond my budget. *She won't be happy.* I climbed the stairs to our bedroom, unsure of what I expected to find, but needing to be able to show Angela I had taken her demands seriously. I stood in silence, closing my eyes, listening out for the scratching sound. Nothing. All I could hear was the sound of the traffic outside as rush hour entered full swing. Then a resounding crash from the other side of the wall, loud enough to startle me. I paused, unsure of what had caused it, but it was soon followed by the sobs of a small child and the muffled voice of her mother.

I gave the skirting boards a cursory glance over, checking for any visible signs of an infestation, of which there were none. *Maybe they were just wiping something off the walls? Perhaps the kid drew on them? If that's the case, then Angela can rest easy, and I've done my bit.* Hesitantly, I made my way back down the stairs and clicked the door on the catch. I stepped over the small wall which separated the two properties and gave the glass pane three sharp knocks. *I should have waited. What if the kid has broken something? They might not be in the mood to talk about rodents.* I cursed my own lack of confidence and waited for a little longer, before knocking again. This time I saw the pink shape of someone growing larger through the frosted glass and was greeted by my frantic looking neighbour.

"Hiya," she said, trying to hide her annoyance at the interruption.

"Hi," I replied. "Sorry to just come around like this."

"It's OK. Millie just pulled her chest of drawers over so I was clearing that up." The woman, whose name I had never been told, looked frazzled; the constant need to supervise a child who was now at an inquisitive age clearly taking a toll.

"Yeah, I heard a bang. Is she alright?"

"Yes, just frightened her. Is that why you came around?" I paused, trying to think of the right words. It was nice that she thought I had been checking up on her daughter's safety, but I would have to admit that it wasn't really my reason for visiting.

"Sort of. Well, no, not really," I explained, awkwardly. "We heard a weird noise last night, like scratching, or scraping. About eleven o'clock. I just wanted to see if you'd been cleaning the walls, or scraping something? It's not a problem," I said quickly, frightened that it would seem as though I was complaining.

"But Angela thinks we have mice in the skirting boards."

"Oh? No, we weren't doing anything like that. Can't say we heard anything, either. I was asleep before ten, but I can ask Mark when he gets home if you want?" Before I could say anything else, we were interrupted by shouts of 'mum' from upstairs, and I took that as my cue to leave.

"Not to worry then," I mumbled as the door closed in my face.

Angela had been home for less than five minutes before she asked how it had gone with the pest-control people. I looked at her with a confused expression. *Did she really think I took time off work, and been able to get them here so quickly?*

"They haven't been out yet," I said.

"Well, when are they coming?"

"I don't know. I didn't call them." I waited for her complaint, but she said nothing, choosing to simply stare at me and wait for me to elaborate. "I've been at work. But I did find the phone number and get a price online," I explained, hoping this would show that I had taken some steps towards dealing with it.

"I guess that's a start." Angela looked as if she wanted me to keep talking.

"And I went next door. They weren't scraping anything, but they didn't hear the noises either. I think we should see what happens tonight; if it happens again I'll call someone out tomorrow." I had no idea how I would pay for it, but it went a small way to easing Angela's worries.

"OK. Make sure you do."

I desperately hoped that all would be quiet when bedtime came around, but it was worse than the night before. Even as we climbed the stairs, we could hear the sound of tiny scratches behind the wooden skirting boards. I dropped to my knees on the laminate flooring, listening intently as I tried to identify the cause. It was as if whatever was behind the glossed whiteness was trying to scratch its way out.

"It sounds trapped in there," I said, once again without thinking.

"Well I don't want something dying in the walls! It will stink the house out." Angela was right, as always.

"So what do you suggest?" I was tired, and growing impatient. I could see that our uninvited guests were about to cause a fight between us.

"You're going to have to take the skirting board off. It only seems to be this one wall." I looked at the floor, weighing up my words before I spoke. Removing the board itself would not be too difficult, and I was confident that I could do it with minimal damage. What put me off was the extremely heavy, five-door, mirrored wardrobe that was in the way.

"Fine," I replied. "But I'll need your help shifting this stuff out of the way." Angela looked at me in disbelief. She was about to protest but decided against it, instead offering to help move the wardrobe, so long as she could leave the room before I pulled the skirting away. Fifteen minutes later, we had piled most of the wardrobe's contents on to our bed and dragged it far enough from the wall to allow me to squeeze behind it. All the activity on our side of the wall must have panicked whatever was within it, and the sounds became louder, more intense, almost disturbing. *Scratch, scratch, scratch.* I told Angela to go and grab my tool box, which she did without complaint. Once I had pulled a mallet and scraper out, she left me to it, hauling a spare duvet from the cupboard and announcing that she would be sleeping on the sofa. I looked at our bed, buried beneath piles of clothes, and knew it would be a late night.

I had no doubt by this point that it was mice. Or, perhaps, rats. The scratching sounds could be heard along the full length of the wall, and I started to grow concerned. *What if I expose a whole bloody nest? There could be hundreds of them in there! A mischief, that's what a group of mice or rats are called. Sounds about bloody right!* Cautiously, I banged the edge of the scraper into the corner of the skirting board, where the two adjacent pieces met. It was louder than I had expected, and I was worried about disturbing next door, but I was more worried about pissing off Angela. Whatever was inside became more frantic at the sound of the banging, desperate to be released. I repeated the action at the other corner, loosening the board at both ends, before starting along the top of the skirting. It was old, and began to come away without too much difficulty. Once I had separated the top of the board from the wood along its entire length, something strange happened. The scratching sound, which had increased to a monumental racket up to this point, stopped. Suddenly, there was silence. I looked towards the bedroom door, debating whether or not to call Angela, but decided against it.

It was only as I grabbed the top of the wood that I noticed how fiercely my hands were trembling. *It's just some bloody mice,* I thought, at least trying to convince myself of that fact. The wood came away with a creak, splitting at the edges a little but largely in one piece. The gap was only a few inches, but the bedroom light was too weak to illuminate it, so I fumbled about in my tool box for a torch. I shone it up and down the gap, the light bouncing around the cobwebs and woodlouse carcasses. Aside from a pair of large house spiders, the space was empty. I scratched at my cheek, puzzled. It made no sense, but I was relieved a swarm of rodents hadn't launched themselves at me and down the stairs.

The sight of the dark opening made me uncomfortable; perhaps it was just the mystery of it all. I was torn between fixing the board back into place and sleeping downstairs, but due to the lateness of the hour, it wasn't much of a choice. I closed the bedroom door, temporarily blocking the scene from my mind, and settled down on the second of our sofas. Angela stirred.

"All sorted?" she mumbled.

"Nothing in there," I told her. She rolled over to face me, almost slipping on to the floor. Her eyes opened a little.

"What was making that noise then?" she asked.

"Must have been next door, I guess. I'll go back around there tomorrow and speak to the guy. See if he knows anything." I tried my best to brush it off, to hide the dread I felt. Something wasn't right, but I needed to keep Angela from getting herself worked up.

I didn't sleep well, unable to get comfortable. Angela seemed to manage, a little to my annoyance. By four in the morning, and after only dozing on and off, I gave up and went upstairs to clear the bed, desperate to get a few hours sleep before work. Grumpily, I threw enough of the clothes into a heap on the floor to clear my side of the bed and crawled in. I was straight out; I enjoyed three full hours of deep sleep before my alarm began to screech. *Nope, too tired,* I decided, certain that I could get away with calling in sick.

The only words I heard from Angela were 'I'm off', to which I mumbled a reply that she would not have been able to hear. I dozed for a large part of the morning, until there came a point at which I knew I had to drag myself out of bed and deal with the mess I had made. It was only as I reached down to scratch an itch on my leg that something felt off, sore even. I yanked away the duvet and recoiled at the sight, leaping into a sitting position and shuffling myself back against the headboard as though trying to distance myself from my own legs. From the edges of my underwear, all the way to my ankles, my legs were bright red with scratches. Angry lines covering the previously white and pasty flesh. Specks of dried blood dotted the sheet and the duvet cover, but most of the scratches had not broken the skin; it was just raised and reddened. The sight of it reminded me of how my back had looked on several occasions when Angela and I had started dating, and the love-making had been much more affectionate than it is now.

I couldn't get my head around it, no matter how hard I tried to come up with an explanation. It looked nothing like an allergic reaction, or heat rash, or even some rare medical condition. I had been furiously scratched, and yet had felt nothing. It made no sense. I scoured the room for some indication as to what could have done this to me but there was nothing; no strands of fur, no tiny footprints, and definitely no horde of rabid mice. I wanted to call Angela, but realized with sadness that she would, most likely, think I was being silly. So instead I set about my tasks, applying wood glue along the skirting board and fixing it back into place. It wasn't a perfect job, but with a touch up of gloss, it was certainly passable. The wardrobe took all my strength to return it to its usual position, but I managed, within a couple of hours, to have the room looking just as it had done the previous day.

I still had not gotten dressed when Angela returned from work, parading about in an old T-shirt and yesterday's underwear. Any other time, she would have made a comment about laziness, or me being a slob, but she was too transfixed on the state of my legs to say anything derogatory.

"What the fuck have you been doing?" she asked, a little angrily, as if I had done this to myself. I explained that I had woken up like this, but that was all the explanation I could offer. I thought she would be frightened, but if she was, then she hid it well. Instead, she looked at me as though I was insane.

"I can't do this any more," she told me. I must have looked as confused as I felt, standing there without speaking. I genuinely did not understand what she meant. "I don't know what's going on with you," she continued. "I only asked you to call a pest-control guy, and you've taken the wall apart, scratched your legs up, you're acting weird. It's like you can't manage a simple task without either doing it wrong or blowing it up into some huge drama." I still didn't understand where she was going with this. "I'm going to get some stuff and stay at my sister's house tonight. We'll talk in a few days." Finally, my mind processed what she had said.

"You're leaving me? Because something scratched my legs?" I shouted, emphasizing how ridiculous that was.

"Quick!" she called from our room. "That sound!" I ran up the stairs to find her, and she was right; the scratching sound was back.

"What the hell?" I wondered aloud.

"Seems pretty obvious to me," she stated, shoving some toiletries into an overnight bag. I stared at her, unable to see what she thought was so clearly a credible explanation. "You can't have looked properly. Some wild thing is in there and must have got to you when you left the board off. Which is *exactly* why I didn't want to sleep in here last night. It probably scurried back in, and now you've trapped it again. Fix it, then we'll talk about where we go from here." With that, she was gone down the stairs and out of the house with a slam of the front door. *Scratch, scratch, scratch.* Something took over me, a rage of some kind, I suppose. I was angry and hurt that Angela could use such a feeble excuse to leave, fed up with the constant criticism from her, disappointed in my own ability to resolve simple problems. Like this fucking scratching. *Scratch, scratch, scratch.*

Angrily, I pulled at the wardrobe, now refilled and heavy, managing to drag it barely six inches from the wall. I kicked at the skirting with my bare feet, which did not damage to the wood but sent a bolt of pain up my leg. I screamed and dropped to the floor. *Scratch, scratch, scratch.* At that moment, I did not care about preserving the skirting board; I had no forethought about the repair job I would need to perform. I wanted that sound to stop, and quickly. Frantically, I pulled a hammer from the tool box and swung it at the wood, causing it to crack. The sound became louder; *scratch, scratch, scratch.* I hit it again, in the same spot. Pieces of wood splintered off, the start of an opening. I struck again and again, moving along the board until I had an opening about a foot long.

Once more, I shone the torch inside and saw nothing but cobwebs and dust. I placed my hands through the hole, gripping the board firmly, and heaved it away, reopening the entire length just as it had been last night. Nothing scurried out; I was greeted only by silence. Using the hammer, I scraped around in the dark, pulling away the webs. Until I hit something. It wasn't something hard, not wood nor brickwork, but soft and living judging by the hiss it let out. I should have moved back, but my rage was in full control; I needed to get the job done, to prove myself to Angela. I reached for the torch and shone it at the place the hammer rested, my face against the floor. Eyes stared back at me; two deep yellow eyes, not dissimilar to a cat's eyes.

But cats do not have hands; long-fingered, withered, grey hands. They tapped their way across the floor towards me before I could react, grabbing my face on both sides. The eyes became larger as they came closer to my own, but the creature's face was hidden in the darkness. For what felt like far too long, we stared at each other, before I tried to pull myself back. I'd lost my strength, or this thing was not as frail as it appeared, and I could not fight it off. Dragged by the head, it took me into its darkness, my eyes and nose filling with dust and rancid cobwebs. I tried to scream but no sound came, only silence. I could not move, fixed into place by the brickwork and the creature, as I felt its fingernails run along my cheeks. My breathing became faster, more panicked, as I tasted the salty skin entering my mouth, fingers exploring the inside of my cheeks. Then, swiftly, there was a sudden bolt of pain as my mouth filled with blood. I tried to spit it out but could not. My eyes widened with terror as I realized that my freshly removed tongue was now blocking my airways.

The police ruled it as 'death by misadventure' after Angela reported it three days later. Of course, she had not heard from me since walking out, which no doubt only enraged her further, and had returned to find out why. And there I was; head rammed into the gap where the skirting board had been, sharp tools all around me and, despite no-one being able to explain how I had actually done it, I had apparently accidentally cut off my own tongue and choked on it. Death by misadventure, or death by stupidity as Angela called it. It took a few days for her to return home, having arranged for the board to be replaced whilst she pretended to grieve at her sister's house. And then it only took a few hours for the sounds to start again; *scratch, scratch, scratch.*

Tunnels

Trick or Treat

"You're all too old to go trick or treating," Mum had told us. "Leave it this year; let the little kids get the sweets. It's not as if Tommy needs to eat any more junk!" She was right about everything, of course. We were too old and Tommy was already heading for a heart attack at the age of fifteen, his diet consisting largely of sausage rolls and fizzy drinks.

"We're still children," I replied, with a smile. "One last time, I promise. Anyway, it's all arranged and I'm meeting some people." I gave mum the innocent look that she could rarely refuse.

"What people?" she asked, studying my face to see if I was about to lie to her.

"Just Chloe and Phoebe. Tommy is walking over with them."

"Like a double-date?" she asked, not looking as though she approved. She strict, and was convinced that any time I would spend time with a girl would end up with her becoming a grandmother.

"Just friends," I told her, and that was the truth, much to my disappointment. I liked both the girls, and so did Tommy. The difference between us was that Tommy didn't stand a chance with either of them, which made things a bit awkward. After muttering something about being safe and not getting up to any mischief, she finally relented and gave her reluctant blessing. Before she could finish laying down the rules, I was already on my way upstairs to get into my costume; a Grim Reaper outfit, complete with a mask and plastic scythe. As a test run I decided to creep up behind my eight-year-old sister, who cried, so I guess it was sufficiently scary for the evening. I picked up my pumpkin-shaped plastic bucket which we had used for years to collect the treats in and told Mum that I was about to leave.

"Have you got your phone?" she asked.

"Nowhere to put it," I explained, running my hands down the sides of the costume to confirm the lack of pockets. "They are meeting me at the end of the road in a few minutes."

"And what if you need to call me?"

"I'm sure they will have phones with them, but we'll be fine." Mum looked worried. She always looked worried.

"OK, back at eight-thirty. That's late enough to be knocking on stranger's doors."

"Nine?" I asked, cheekily.

"Eight forty-five, and not a minute after." I lifted my mask to give her a peck on the cheek and ran out of the house, my black costume flapping behind me.

Tommy and the girls all lived on the same road, about a ten-minute walk from me. Without wanting to sound snobbish, it is a fact that my house is on the nicer side of town. This is why we planned to knock on doors near mine; apparently, some of the houses over their way weren't very friendly. This also made things easier with my Mum, knowing that I would be close by. I stood at the corner of the road feeling a little foolish in my costume, waiting for the others who were late as always. The thinness of the material provided little barrier against the cold wind, and I shivered, beginning to get impatient. I tried to construct a logical route in my head that would reap the most reward, but my thoughts were quickly interrupted by the sound of giggling coming from behind me. Tommy was wearing his usual clothes; blue jeans and a football shirt which did not completely cover his belly. The extent of his Halloween efforts consisted of some white face paint with a couple of red lines, which I presumed to represent blood.

The girls, on the other hand, had put in a lot of effort, and I was thankful that mum had not seen them. They wore matching, white nurses' uniforms. Their faces were painted green and looked zombie-like; I guess girls are good at the face paint and make-up side of things. Far better than Tommy, anyway. The uniforms were short, almost up to their buttocks, and red, fishnet stockings did little to cover the exposed flesh. I tried not to stare, but it wasn't easy.

"Where do you want to start?" I asked. "I thought we'd do my road and then the houses up towards the church; they're usually pretty good." The others laughed, looking at each other as if they had a secret. "What?" I asked, not understanding what was funny.

"The girls want to check out the Monroe house," Tommy stated, a mischievous grin on his face. He knew how I'd respond.

"Are you serious?" I asked, looking at the girls.

"Don't be a baby," Phoebe replied, taking my hand. As much as it felt like a terrible idea, peer-pressure and a pretty girl made my mind up for me. The Monroe house was isolated, being situated on the edge of a large, green, public space, out of sight of any other houses. Dog walkers were pretty much the only people to ever pass the house, and rarely after dark. At this time of the year, the Monroe house went all-out for Halloween, with elaborate decorations adorning the front garden and exterior of the house. None of us had met anyone who had actually seen someone living at the house, and this had sparked a range of playground rumours. Of course, the house was haunted, no-one dared to refute that out loud (although I doubted that it was the case). Only Max, a boy from school who was in the year above us, claims to have been there last Halloween.

"You don't actually believe Max's nonsense about knocking there before, do you?" I said, as we made our way past rows of terraced houses with pumpkins in the windows.

"It's probably bullshit," Tommy said, starting to feel a little nervous as we approached the darkness of the dirt track.

"Yeah, maybe. In which case there's no harm having a look," Phoebe said, squeezing my hand. "And what if he was telling the truth?" Max's version, which is highly debatable, was that he had knocked on the door of the Monroe house, bravely by himself, calling out trick or treat. Although he didn't see anyone, Max told everyone around the school that some wrinkly fingers with long nails had pushed a fifty-pound note out of the letter box. He had stood staring at it in disbelief when the three full-sized skeletons that were decorating the garden turned to face him. He insists that they chased him away, and as much as everyone laughed at him, no-one dared to go there and find out for themselves. Hence, the legend began.

Part of me hoped the house would not have been decorated, that the lights would be off, that we would decide not to knock. I'm sure we all gasped a little as we turned the corner from the track and gazed upon the Monroe house. Three plastic skeletons were erected in the garden, positioned with shovels around a hole in the ground. A hole which looked to be the right size to bury a body. There were tacky decorations in all the front-facing windows; strings of lights with ghosts and pumpkins, decals of witches on the glass, and a light-up sign attached to the front door which read 'enter if you dare!'.

"It looks pretty cool," Chloe said.

"Guess so," I muttered, my eyes fixed on the skeletons, just in case they moved. Which they didn't, of course.

"Give the door a knock then," Tommy ordered, from his position about six feet behind the rest of us. "Let's get this fifty quid, and we'll go somewhere else." I looked at him as if he were an idiot. We were gathered by the small gate which opened on to the property, no-one wanting the take the lead. After a series of awkward glances had been exchanged, Chloe huffed and walked through the gate.

"If no-one else comes to the door, then the money is all mine," she stated, turning to face us. Again, Phoebe gripped my hand tighter and followed her friend toward the door, dragging me with her. Chloe banged on the door, three loud knocks echoed throughout the house. We were greeted by silence.

"No-one home," I declared with relief, turning to leave. Chloe knocked again. This time we heard footsteps, accompanied by a kind of dragging sound; the first image to come to mind was a heavy-set person dragging a body. We all took a step back and waited, suddenly hopeful that some money would be pushed through the letterbox after all. However, it wasn't; the only sound was that of numerous locks being undone. I wanted to leave at this point, but I was also frightened to run away after we had disturbed whoever lived there.

When the last locked clicked, there was a pause. I wondered if the resident was elderly and had changed their mind about opening the door. Then, with a creak, it began to swing open.

"Trick or treat," Chloe announced, trying to sound friendly. There was no-one there, just a dark hallway barely illuminated by a string of fairy lights of either side. "Hello?" she called into the house.

"Probably a good time to leave," I said, no longer caring if my friends thought I was a wimp. There was no-one there and walking in would be trespassing.

"Hello?" Chloe called again, this time placing one foot across the threshold.

"You can come in!" came a voice, startling us all. It sounded as though it belonged to an old woman.

"Sorry if we disturbed you," I called in response, whispering to the others once again that we should leave.

"It's no bother," the voice replied. "I've got some Halloween treats here, if that is what you were after? Just in the hallway, help yourself. Sorry I can't bring them out; I'm a bit frail these days."

"See! It's fine," Chloe said, not sounding entirely convinced.

"Seriously?" Tommy said, a little more loudly than he had intended. "She could make it to the door to open it, so why didn't she bring the treats then?" He had a point. The temptation of money, or even some other decent reward got the better of us and each holding on to one another, we crept into the hallway.

"Leave the door open," I told Tommy, who looked at me as if to say that was the most obvious thing in the world.

"I've set up a Halloween game in the hallway if you want to play?" asked the voice. "Do a trick, get a treat. I hope you enjoy it." It was creepy, and I was beyond having second thoughts. I decided that we should see the Monroe woman, at least show our faces, so I walked into the dark room that the voice came from.

"Hello?" No reply. I fumbled for a light switch. It didn't work.

"The power must be off," Tommy suggested.

"The fairy lights are working," I said, pointing to the plug sockets that they were attached to.

"Bulb must have gone, then," he said.

"Hello?" I called again, moving further into the room. Nothing. My eyes adjusted to the dark a little and there was no doubt that the room was empty. I felt colder. Something was wrong. "I'm going," I told them, turning back towards the door. Before anyone could answer me, the door slammed shut, the bolts' locking of their own accord. Chloe screamed. Phoebe began to cry.

"What the fuck?" Tommy declared. He ran to the door, attempting to pull back the bolts but found them to be red hot; the tips of two fingers and his thumb now blistered. "Fucking hell!"

"I don't like this," Phoebe said, between sobs.

"Call someone," I suggested. "I left my phone at home." The three of them all pulled their phones out of bags and pockets. No signal on any of them; not phone signal or Internet coverage. The only option for us was to look for another way out. From the outside, we saw two large windows on the ground floor, with the hallway being central to the house. The living room that we had investigated was on our left; there should have been a door to the right but the wall was solid. There were three, front-facing windows on the first floor, but we could not see any stairs as we approached the end of the hallway. It was dark, but I could sense the dread that the others were feeling, hear the sobs that Phoebe tried to stifle.

"We'll have to smash the living room window and climb out," Tommy suggested, his voice rising in panic. Unable to think of anything else, we walked back along the corridor only to discover that there was now no door on either side. We returned to the entrance, to find the locks still white-hot. We were trapped, completely walled in. Chloe flicked on the flashlight app on her phone. The only items in the hallway were two boxes, each about two feet cubed. One was labelled tricks'; the other was labelled treats'. Tommy opened the treats' box as Chloe shone her light into it. It was empty. Cautiously, the pair opened the tricks' box. There were five black envelopes in the box, each numbered, beginning at one. Tommy picked up the first and opened it, pulling the card from inside. As he read it, he couldn't help smiling and, for a brief moment, I thought everything was going to be OK.

"What's it say?" I asked.

"It says," Tommy began, "that when we complete the trick card, we will get a treat card."

"But the box was empty."

"Yeah, well the bloody living room was there a moment ago."

"And what is the trick?"

"It says we have to kiss each other." Tommy was smirking.

"Oh, piss off!" Phoebe said. "You're making that up. It's hardly the time for joking about." Tommy showed us the card, and he was right; 'Kiss the other members of your group'. It sounded simple enough. We all looked at each other, a little uneasily. Then Phoebe kissed me, full on the mouth. My teenage brain kicked in, and I kissed her back, not wanting to waste the opportunity. When she eventually pulled away, we looked at Tommy and Chloe. He wore a huge grin, but she looked as though she would vomit.

"It'll be fine," Phoebe told her, as if trying to prepare her for an unpleasant ordeal. They kissed, awkwardly and quickly, before opening the treats' box once again. Empty.

"I read the card, so maybe I have to kiss both of you," Tommy said, winking at Phoebe in the dark. She didn't hesitate, and having nothing better to suggest, kissed him on the mouth. Still no treat, unless you count the pleasure Tommy was getting from it all.

"Or maybe you have to kiss <u>everyone</u>," Chloe suggested, looking a little pleased with herself. It took me a moment to realize what she meant.

"Nope!" I said, without hesitation.

"It's no more gross than us having to kiss him," Chloe told me.

"Thanks!" Tommy replied. "Come here, big boy!" he said to me, trying to make light of the situation.

"OK, but no tongues," I warned him. He didn't listen, finding the whole thing funny as he slipped his tongue into my mouth. I leapt back in disgust. Chloe was right. He had needed to kiss us all, and there was now a treat envelope to open.

"Ten pounds," Tommy announced as he pulled it from the envelope and stuffed it into his pocket.

"To split," Chloe said.

"It was my card!" he retorted.

"You were the only one enjoying it; we should be paid for having to kiss you!"

"Like a prostitute?" Tommy replied, smugly. Chloe stopped talking after that.

"We can worry about that if we get out of here. Who is going to open the second trick?"

"I'll do another," Tommy offered. "Maybe I'll get a hand-job this time."

"I'd rather die," Chloe said. "I'll do it." Handing the phone to Tommy to hold, she read the second card aloud. "Slap the other members of your group." With an idea of the rules, and no restraint, Chloe smacked Tommy across the face, hard. He yelped and looked angry but kept his mouth shut. She proceeded to slap me, not with much force, and then Phoebe, muttering an apology as she did it. Quickly, she turned to the treats' box and pulled out the new envelope, stuffing the twenty-pound note into the top of her stockings.

"Now you really look like a whore," Tommy told her. She ignored him. "Who's next?" He looked at Phoebe and I. I let her choose and, with the assumption that the tricks would become more severe, she asked to go next. After I had nodded, she opened the box, taking out the third envelope and reading it in her head. Her eyes widened a little, and she looked at us nervously.

"I'm not doing that," she said, holding the card to her chest. "Let's check the door again, maybe we can touch the locks with something over our hands?"

"Like what?" Tommy asked. "You two are pretty much naked and that Grim Reaper outfit looks like it'd burst into flames." Phoebe headed to the door regardless, and we heard a clink as she slid one of the bolts aside. I ran over to her in excitement.

"Have they cooled down?"

"Only the bottom two. You can feel the heat from the other four."

"Two cards, two locks," I muttered as our eyes met. "We're going to have to do all of them."

"But there are five cards and six locks," she pointed out.

"Maybe the last treat is the final bolt?" I said, hopefully. "What did your card say?" She passed it to me and looked at the floor. 'Take blood from the other members of your group'. Attached to the card with some tape was a razor blade.

"It's fine," I told her, putting my hands on her shoulders. "I'm sure just a drop will be enough; it won't hurt." I unstuck the blade and handed it to her, extending my fingers in front of her. "Just prick the end." It stung like a paper cut, quickly turning crimson as a few drops fell from the end of my forefinger. Tommy and Chloe were still bickering and hadn't heard what we needed to do. Perhaps the strangeness of the situation had gotten to them, but they did not try to refuse. After all, what else could we have done. Phoebe went to the door to check our theory out and found three bolts were now cool enough to handle. In the treat box was an envelope containing a fifty-pound note.

"I guess I'm up next," I said, moving towards the box.

"Shit, sorry," Tommy mumbled, holding card number four in his hands. "I've just read it." He didn't look happy. I snatched it from him; 'Choose one member of the group to leave behind'.

"Well I don't see what you're meant to do, it's not as if we can get out yet," I told him.

"And we aren't leaving anyone behind!" Chloe said, panicking that Tommy would choose her. I opened the treat box but found nothing. We were puzzled, not understanding what was required of us.

"Just pick someone and say the words," Phoebe suggested. "As long as we all understand that we don't really leave anyone here." We all nodded.

"I choose Chloe to leave behind," Tommy announced, loudly. Chloe slapped him for a second time, muttering 'prick' under her breath. "Easy money," Tommy said, tearing at the fourth envelope. "This is becoming quite profitable," he said, holding up eighty pounds with a greedy grin. He added the money to his earlier 'prize', and then it happened. Perhaps it was a delay from him saying the words, maybe it needed him to actually pocket the cash, but that was confirmation enough. A swirling pattern began to appear on the wall behind Chloe. Before we could warn her, six arms reached out as far as the elbow, wrapping around our friend. She let out a muffled scream, but it was too late; they pulled her into the wall, and she was gone. Too quickly for us to react, too suddenly for us to even process what was happening. Phoebe launched herself at Tommy, pounding his huge gut with punches. He felt responsible, that much was obvious, but she was gone and there was no obvious way to get her back.

"One more card," I said. "Let's get this done and get out. We can find help once we escape this house." I picked up the final card, ignoring my apprehension. I just wanted this to be over with. Inside the envelope was a small rubber stamp and ink; the sort of thing you find in gift shops at tourist attractions. I opened it to see a skull design. 'Choose one member of the group to play with the skeletons.'

"That doesn't sound like something any of us want to do," Phoebe said. "Remember Max said those things in the garden chased him."

"If that's the case, then I should choose myself; I'm most likely to be able to outrun them."

"What if you can't? Or if that isn't what it means?" We both looked at Tommy.

"Do whatever," he said, not seeming to care. "If those bony fuckers try anything then I'll sit on them." He was trying to sound brave, but his voice quivered as he spoke. It was selfish of me, but he had done that to Chloe so it felt fair. If I had to choose between Tommy and Phoebe then there was no choice at all. I walked over and stamped a red skull on Tommy's forehead.

"That was the last card," I pointed out, opening the treats' box. There was a larger envelope; thick and padded. From inside I pulled out a card with a grinning clown, and a thick glove. I stared at it for a moment. Heatproof, I told myself, slipping it on. We ran to the door, pulling across the last of the bolts and yanking it open. Outside was dark, but nothing like what we had been enclosed within. As we stepped into the fresh air, our path was blocked by the grave-digging skeletons, heads cocked to one side as they surveyed us. We froze, just for a moment. Then something registered with them as they seemed to notice the stamp on Tommy's head. It happened in the briefest of moments; he was surrounded and all three, simultaneously, extended their bony hands. They jabbed at Tommy's belly with such speed that they became a blur, the white bones turning red in the spray. Tommy's eyes were wide, his mouth gurgling blood as he dropped to the ground. We didn't try to help him, it was too late, so we ran. Phoebe and I, together, leaving our friend to be dragged into the freshly dug earth.

The house was deserted when we came back with help. There were no decorations, no old lady, just dust and empty rooms. The doors were where they should have been, as were the stairs. It was as if nothing had happened, and it was just us playing a Halloween prank. Of course, Chloe and Tommy were never found, and we were under scrutiny regarding their disappearances but no-one could prove anything. The only person that believed us was Max, who had actually had company when he visited the Monroe house last year, but had been too afraid to mention the disappearance of his older brother. A year later and Max's parents still think their oldest child is travelling the world.

Tunnels

Ghost hunters. Just another group of fraudsters along with psychics, witch doctors and faith healers. As much as I enjoyed a good scary story, I had no doubts that this was all it was; just a story. Even so, fear had an appeal; the adrenalin was addictive. Between my wife and I, we had seen almost every horror film worth watching, and many that weren't. We'd read countless tales of vengeful ghosts, demonic possession, psychotic killers, and zombie infestations. Then came the immersive experiences which have exploded in popularity over the past few years.

Our first was a Halloween horror show on a farm; essentially a walk-through filled with actors whose job it was to terrify the visitors. This initial experience blew us away, leaving us desperate for more. We attended theatrical murder mystery events and frightening team games, which involved solving puzzles to escape 'certain death'. We screamed our way through the city's old dungeons, and even attended a weekend of 'zombie outbreak survival' training.

It became a hobby, of sorts, and we were constantly searching for the next horrifying experience. Sometimes we would drive for hours to try out a new attraction, listening to creepy audio books on the journey to set the mood. We'd been face-to-face with killer clowns, living scarecrows, and more than a handful of zombies. We'd been startled by bumps in the night, and had literally run away from a chainsaw-wielding maniac. The only thing that did not hold any interest, to me at least, were ghosts. Pretend ghostly effects were fine; what I could not understand were events which claimed to be able to show you real ghosts. Confident in my belief that they did not exist, I saw no appeal in spending the night being guided down damp passageways, only to have my beliefs confirmed, and to have to pay for the privilege.

My wife, however, had always believed in ghosts; which may explain why she usually found these things more frightening than I did, and why after a particularly well-done ghost film, she would need me to accompany her to the bathroom, turning on every light on the way. She was regularly pointing out these ghost-hunting events, and I was invariably ignoring her not-so-subtle hints; until one came up at a venue within walking distance of our home. The poster invited people to explore 'the famously haunted tunnels of the wartime fort', a structure which was, perhaps, a mile from our house at most. We had visited the fort on numerous occasions, to look around the museum and enjoy a coffee, but we had never been there after dark.

"Famously haunted?" I said, with a disapproving look. "Can't be that famous."

"We have to go!" Lily demanded, a serious look on her face. "Plus, you owe me for that last place we went to."

"What place?" I asked, despite knowing full-well what she meant. It was advertised with all the usual buzzwords; terrifying, shocking, horrific and so on. But it was also being touted as 'next-level'; claiming previous visitors had left screaming as it was just 'too intense'. Unfortunately, it turned out to simply be a field in the middle of nowhere, full of terrible actors running around, struggling not to laugh themselves. I smiled at the memory; it had been so awful that it now seemed funny. Lily did not agree, and just looked at me. I sighed.

"Fine. On one condition."

"Hmm?"

"If we don't find any ghosts, then we don't go on another ghost hunt again."

"OK, deal."

"And..." I continued. "And we find a secluded bit of the tunnels to get frisky in." There was a pause as I waited for Lily to laugh my suggestion off, but she didn't.

"I'll wear a skirt then," she announced, a coy smile appearing on her red lips.

When the day arrived, I did not feel anything like my normal level of enthusiasm. I was more tired than usual, and the thought of going through empty tunnels until three in the morning on a cold, drizzly night was not at all appealing.

"You still want to go tonight?" I asked.

"Of course. I can't wait!" Lily replied. "Don't be wimping out on me now."

"I'm not. It's just going to be a late one, and I'm tired already."

"So, have a nap before we go. I'm still going, even if you don't come. And if you still want this..." Lily said, lifting her skirt high enough to reveal the black lace beneath. I gasped, involuntarily.

"I can't say no to that," I told her, trying to shift the reluctant feeling I had about the evening. I was not tired enough to sleep during the day, but spent the afternoon lounging on the sofa, watching old vampire films from the 1960s while Lily pottered around the house.

"Should we take anything with us?" she asked, popping her head around the living room door. It was getting dark outside, and I still had little motivation to move from where I lay.

"Like what?"

"I don't know. I have the tickets in my bag, but wondered if we should take torches? Or drinks?"

"Both would be good; I suppose. Even just for getting back afterward, a torch would be useful; it's a dark walk from the fort to the main road in the middle of the night. Will you be warm enough in that skirt?"

"I'll be fine. I'll take a hat and coat - you should do the same." Lily walked out of the room, leaving me to continue staring at the television, watching as a vampire sank his teeth into the neck of young virgin, all played out in black and white. Soon, Lily returned carrying two torches. She clicked them both on at the same time, right into my eyes.

"Jesus!" I muttered.

"They work!" she declared. "And I have spare batteries in my bag. Get yourself ready, it's almost time!" she squealed, barely able to hide her excitement. As I pulled on my walking boots, Lily handed me a water bottle. I stared at the bubbles drifting to the surface.

"It's fizzy," I pointed out, dryly.

"Gin and tonic. It is Friday night, after all."

Linking arms, we made our way out into the cool air of the small town. It was peaceful outside, but with enough of a chill for our breath to become visible as we exhaled. The air felt damp, not really raining, but wet enough to make Lily's bare legs glisten with goose bumps. Despite it being Friday evening, the town was small, and we barely passed anyone else on the fifteen-minute walk to the fort. I glanced at my watch; it was eight thirty-five and we were almost there.

"We're going to be early," I pointed out.

"Better than being late. Plus the tour starts at nine; we don't want to miss anything."

"How on earth is it going to take six hours to walk around the tunnels? The place isn't that big!"

"I suppose," Lily said with a smirk, "that it depends on what we find down there!"

"Probably nothing," I muttered. Either Lily didn't hear me, or she chose to ignore my negativity, but she did not respond. As we turned away from the main road on to the path which led up to the fort's entrance, Lily began to rummage through her bag for the torches. It was cold, and I was growing impatient.

"How much crap have you got in there?" I moaned, knowing all too well that her bag was like a bottomless pit, filled with an eclectic mix of supposedly essential items.

"Here we go," she announced, passing me one of the torches. "Let's go get spooked!" I smiled a little at her childlike enthusiasm, as she stood in front of me with her torch pointing upwards beneath her chin, illuminating her pretty face. She looked as though she were about to tell a scary story around a campfire.

"I'm just here for the black lace," I told her, giving her bottom a playful squeeze.

"Then you'd better not let the poltergeists get to me first!" We made our way up the path, thick trees forming a barrier on either side of us. It was dark, but the light from the almost-full moon would have nearly sufficed if we had had no torches. Barely twenty feet from the gated entrance, we heard the first scream of the evening; a high-pitched squeal of someone genuinely petrified. We both paused for a moment until we heard laughter following it. I sighed with relief, assuming that someone already inside had fallen victim to a prank of some kind. At least, I hoped that was what had happened.

We were greeted at the gates by the two organizers; Matthew and Chloe. They wore matching hooded tops, which bore the details of their business. I took this as evidence, if any were even needed, that this was purely a money-making venture. Of course, all the immersive events we had attended were businesses of some kind, but they never pretended to be anything other than that. These guys were trying to peddle some truth behind their ghost stories, and that was what had my back up.

Matthew was short, or Chloe was tall; it was difficult to tell from our position on the other side of the gate, in the dark. Either way, they were the same height. They were also both a little overweight and wore nearly identical glasses. In the blackness of the evening, it would have been quite possible to mistake one of them for the other, especially in their matching, branded, baseball caps. I wondered for a moment if they were siblings, or lovers. Then I pondered the idea that they were both, and I felt a little queasy.

"Good evening ghost hunters!" Matthew said, much more loudly than was necessary. The pair of them had unsettling grins across their faces, signalling, to me anyway, that we were about to be taken for a ride by these over-confident fraudsters.

"So, you've got ghosts here then?" I asked, making no attempt to hide my skepticism. Lily nudged me, as if I were embarrassing her already. As our guides removed the padlocked chain and proceeded to open up the wrought-iron gates, Lily pulled out the ticket confirmation that I had printed that morning. Once they had scrutinized the tickets, Matthew and Chloe welcomed us to what they promised would be 'a truly terrifying tour of one of the south coast's most haunted locations', and led us to the open space at the centre of the fort. Neither of them had answered my question about ghosts, barely seeming to acknowledge that I had even spoken. I was certain that I had offended them already, but did not particularly care; after all, I was on the gin and knew they were running a scam. Which is why I asked again.

"Is it just the one ghost? Or is there a whole family down there?" Chloe looked me in the eye, the grin falling away from her face, realizing that she was being mocked.

"There is no doubt that there are at least three spirits dwelling in the deeper tunnels, directly beneath where we are standing right now. It is quite possible that there are more. Hopefully, you will get to meet some of them tonight." Before I could respond, Chloe turned away and taking Matthew by the hand, the pair climbed on to a lone picnic table which stood outside of the small, now closed, coffee shop.

"Welcome everybody," Matthew began. There was a faint murmur from the other patrons. I looked around and counted another five people, beside myself and Lily. They had all been talking together when we had approached so it was impossible to tell if they had booked as one group or simply struck up a conversation on arrival.

"Before we begin, I need to go over some ground rules for everyone's safety," Matthew said, his voice beginning to sound more theatrical. "In the case of an emergency, the only exit is through the gates which you came in by. It was a working fort at one time and would therefore have been rather foolish to feature emergency exits!" He laughed a little at what he saw as his clever joke. No-one else laughed. "Anyway, the gates are currently locked, but both myself and Chloe have keys; feel free ask either of us if you need to leave before the end." The gin was starting to go to my head, and the guy stood on the picnic table was irritating me, so I decided to ask a question.

"What if something happens to both of you, and we can't get the keys to get out?"

"I can assure you that won't be an issue," Matthew said with a smile. "We have dealt with many spirits in the past, some of which were rather aggressive, and we would not put any of you, or ourselves, in real danger."

"Of course," I muttered sarcastically.

"It is imperative," Matthew continued, "that we all stay together. I will take the lead, and Chloe will take up the rear." I sniggered, immaturely. Lily nudged me again. "You are welcome to take photographs, and we have extra torches if anyone needs one," our guide explained. "It is, of course, very dark in the tunnels and there are a lot of steep steps. Before I pass over to Chloe for a bit of history on the place, does anyone need to use the toilet?" No-one spoke. "Very well. Chloe will explain the legend of the haunting here, and then we'll be on our way."

"I'm going for a wee," I whispered to Lily, as soon as Chloe began speaking.

"OK."

"Wanna come?" I asked. Her eyes widened in mock surprise.

"I'm fine, thanks. Don't worry, you'll get your chance later with me. Now shh, I want to hear the story." With a little huff, I made my way back to the iron gates, next to which were the toilets. I dawdled as best I could, managing to miss the first half of Chloe's speech much to my relief. As I resumed my position next to Lily, I was just in time to hear about the three spirits which were supposedly haunting the tunnels.

"She had been a powerful witch, strong enough to place Henry Oats, a wealthy landowner, under her spell. He owned the land on which we are standing now, with his wife Clara, and daughter Elizabeth. The story goes that Henry was seduced by the witch, and caught in the act of love-making, by his wife. Clara was devastated, fleeing from the family home, only to be crushed to death outside by a falling oak. Was it a freak accident, or was it witchcraft?" Chloe looked at our small gathering, as if expecting an answer.

"Was it windy that night?" I asked. "Trees do blow over." I heard someone giggle from the other group, but Chloe chose to continue her tale.

"It was a still night, with no wind or any record of a storm." Chloe stared at me as she said this.

"She's just made that bit up," I whispered to Lily, who ignored me.

"Of course no-one could prove that the witch was responsible for Clara's death, but there were suspicions among the locals. Henry seemed to take his wife's passing well, quickly moving his new lover into his home, enrolling her as a step-mother to little Elizabeth. The child had only been five years old when her mother had died, but she suspected foul play. Unable to understand her father's obsession with this strange woman, and his indifference to her mother's death, Elizabeth eventually sought help from officials in the nearest town. Despite the oddness of Clara's death, Elizabeth's concerns were chalked up to simply disliking her step-mother. This was until people started dying. Over the space of a year, there were a number of other freak accidents; falling trees, unexplained drownings, a shock suicide, and even the unfortunate case of a rich widow falling face-first into a fire. It did not take much digging to find a link between each of the newly deceased; they had all owned land which bordered onto Henry's, or was very near to it. They had all, also, refused to sell it to him. Once this connection was established, the townsfolk were up in arms, angry, and thirsty for revenge. Henry was sleeping when the mob descended on his house, but Elizabeth was at the door, ready to let them in. The mob would not wait for a trial, fearful that the witch would use magic to escape, and she was sentenced to death by fire as soon as they had dragged her into the town square. Henry stayed at the house, powerless to help the woman, unwilling to watch her death in person. Elizabeth, however, wanted to see for herself that the witch was gone. Standing barely six feet away, her eyes met the witch's. Elizabeth watched the flames, oblivious to the cart behind her. She did not see its wheel hit a hole in the road, causing a barrel to fall. She did not see that barrel roll at her from behind. All she felt was herself falling forward into the flames. No-one from the crowd dared try to pull her out, too afraid that the barrel of gunpowder would explode." Chloe paused, perhaps in an attempt to create drama.

"And did it?" one of the girls called out.

"Yes it did. The witch and Elizabeth were killed instantly. Shall we begin the tour?"

"Hang on," the girl called out again, an almost finished cigarette in her gloved hand. She was a little older than us, with dyed black hair, long dark coat, black lipstick, the works. "So, what happened to Henry?"

"No-one knows for sure," Chloe said. "He became a recluse, presumably devastated by the loss of his family. He died at the house, but there is no cause of death listed in the records."

"So, you're saying the three spirits here are Henry, Elizabeth and the witch? What about Clara? And the other people that the witch killed?" the goth woman asked.

"Perhaps they're all down there!" Matthew interjected. "Elizabeth likes to run along the narrow corridors, singing." At this point, Lily held my arm, a look of wonder on her face.

"I hope we get to see a ghost!" she whispered, excitedly.

"Let's hope it's Henry then," I told her, going along with the story. "Kids creep me out at the best of times, and that witch sounds like a right bitch!"

Matthew and Chloe led us to a door in the north-east corner of the fort; the entrance to a system of narrow tunnels which connected the various rooms. When the fort had been in use during the second world war, these rooms had been used to store ammunition and supplies for the soldiers stationed there. Once the door had been closed behind us, something which felt unnecessary, it was beyond simply being dark. It was now pitch black and if we had not had the torches, we would not have been able to see someone standing right in front of us. Lily clung on to me as we made our way down the first set of steep, concrete steps, half-expecting an actor to jump out on us at any moment. There was nothing. Our guides led us to the left as we reached the bottom of the steps, into a small room with candle-powered lanterns adorning the walls.

"If everyone can take a seat please, we will make our first attempt to establish contact with any spirits present, before we move on any farther," Matthew ordered. I looked across at the row of plastic, green chairs lined against one wall; eight of them. In front of the chairs stood a table with a Ouija board on it. When we had all taken our seats, I watched intently as Matthew played his part, eyes closed, moving things around on the board. He called out loudly to the spirits of Elizabeth and Henry, almost begging for them to reveal themselves to the group. Nothing. Then Matthew fixed his gaze straight at me. "Everyone needs to hold hands or this will not work," he said, unable to conceal his annoyance as he glanced at my right hand. Instead of holding Lily's, as we had been told to, I had rested it just beneath her skirt, touching her thigh. Under the stare of everyone, I removed my hand from its inappropriate location and took Lily's. Matthew began to call upon the spirits once more. This time something did happen; all eight of the lanterns went out simultaneously. The whole group, myself included, gasped, largely due to the sudden darkness that we had been plunged into. There was a nervous laugh as everyone fumbled with their torches. Our hosts did a good job at looking worried, as if they had not been responsible for the lights going out. I shone my torch towards the ceiling, looking for something that would give away the trick, but found nothing.

"That was pretty cool," I admitted to Lily, a little annoyed that I couldn't figure out how it had been done.

"Where's the blonde girl?" I heard someone ask. Turning to my left, I looked down the row of seats to see that Chloe was sat at the far end. The chair next to her now sat empty. The man who had asked the question stood up, looking around, puzzled. He had been sat to her right.

"What do you mean blonde girl?" the goth asked. "I thought you two were together."

"Nope, I came on my own. Looks like she did too."

"Were you not holding her hand?" Matthew asked, looking concerned.

"I was, but she let go as soon as the lights went out."

"Bravo!" I declared. I couldn't help myself laughing at this point. "So, one of the guests disappears, one who happened to come here alone, and who happened to be sitting next to Chloe at the time. You know there's a passageway at that end of the room, right?" The others stood to have a look. I was right, of course, having been in the tunnels before. The passageway entrance was indented into the wall in the far corner and could easily go unnoticed. Everyone seemed to relax, seeing the hoax for what it was. Everyone apart from Matthew and Chloe, who just exchanged worried glances.

"What's her name?" goth girl asked, looking to Chloe. "We should call her back." Chloe looked to Matthew, unsure of how to answer.

"She wasn't with us," Matthew said. "I don't want to cause any panic, but she honestly did come alone, as a paying customer like the rest of you."

"Bullshit," I announced, but I was beginning to doubt my own confidence. The two hosts looked far more worried than anyone else.

"Then maybe she just thought it would be funny," said the guy who had been sat next to her when she disappeared. "Sure she'll be back soon."

"I hope so," goth girl said. "But it was you that put out the candles, wasn't it?" she said, looking nervously at Matthew.

"You came for a ghost hunt; don't start to freak out when you actually encounter one." He seemed to have lost his friendliness, however fake it had been, and now appeared on edge, as though he had made a mistake.

"He's got a point." I turned to see Lily standing up, addressing the group. "Whether we honestly thought we would have some kind of paranormal encounter or not, we all came for the frights. We've been to a lot of things like this, and this one doesn't seem much different. Matthew and Chloe are in character, and are unlikely to break that unless there is an actual emergency. Whether blondie was an actress, or she thought it would be funny to hide of her own accord, is neither here nor there. The point is, we had a scare, and now we move on to the next part of the tour; isn't that right?" She looked at Matthew, desperately wanting her words to be true.

"Erm," he stuttered, glancing at Chloe, "Yes. That's right. And as someone said, I'm sure the other guest will reappear in due course. Probably quite soon, in fact, as that passageway is where we're heading next." Matthew shone his torch into the narrow entrance, failing to hide his hesitance. "It's a squeeze in here, but this is where the soldiers used to bring the stores of food. There are numerous small store rooms, which come off of the passageway. It is also the location of the most frequent sightings of Elizabeth, so keep your eyes peeled."

Four of the group followed behind Matthew, torches flickering to cast as much light as possible in the tight space. I followed, with Lily close behind. I could feel her grabbing on to the back of my jacket. The walls were no more than a foot and a half apart, causing one of the larger guests to turn a little to the side as he walked. No-one spoke, the only sounds being those of heavy breathing and the scraping of clothing along the damp walls as we made our way along. We passed the first two store rooms, one on either side of the passageway. When we reached the entrance to the third, Matthew halted the line.

"If everyone could come in to this room please; I have another little story to share with you." We all shuffled in, and it was a relief to see some large electric lights attached to the wall. The brightness was a little dazzling, but certainly made us all feel safer. Everyone turned off their torches, all except Lily, who pointed hers at the floor as if preparing for another blackout.

"Everyone still here?" I asked, glancing around. Eight people; still one less than we started with but no new surprises. Yet. The group murmured as if to confirm their presence and Matthew began to talk, summoning his theatrical voice once again.

"This room is a key part to the story of Henry Oats. It lies directly beneath the location of his home. During our research, we were told by several eyewitnesses, that an image of a bearded man had appeared in this very room on numerous occasions. He did not seem menacing, so please do not be afraid. I will call out to him, and perhaps he will make an appearance." Matthew began calling Henry's name, asking him to make his presence known, but to no avail. The next ten seconds were a blur, however. The electric lamps all went out, again plunging us into darkness, aside from the light from Lily's torch. Everyone made some kind of sound, ranging from a slight gasp to a full-blown scream. Then there was laughter and the room was illuminated again. As I looked toward the sound of the laughter, I saw that it was coming from the man who had been sat next to the blonde lady. He was in hysterics, his hand still resting on the switch for the lighting.

"Fucking arsehole!" the goth girl said.

"I'm sorry; I couldn't resist," the man said, still laughing at his prank. The entire group was looking at him, trying not to give him the satisfaction of actually having terrified all of us. Which is why the whole group saw his face change, from a self-satisfied smirk to pure fear. His eyes widened. His jaw fell slack, as he gazed beyond us. Lily was behind me and as she turned, was the first to let out a scream. Chloe had been stood in the entrance to the room; well, she still was. But now she was merely propped up against the concrete wall. Her eyes bulged, looking as though they would jump from their sockets at any moment. Her skin had turned a paler shade, and her trousers were dark from urine. We all stared for a moment, trying to process the image, trying to persuade ourselves that it was just part of the show. But there was no mistaking that Chloe was dead, the bottom of her torch protruding from her widened mouth, the shaft of it rammed down her throat.

The group parted to allow Matthew through, who tearfully lowered her to the floor. He struggled to pull the torch free, and it came out with the crack of a tooth. He looked stunned, as if he did not know what he was now required to do.

"This is your fault!" he suddenly yelled at the man who'd turned off the lights, before lunging towards him. Matthew shoved him against the wall, before breaking down in tears. It was clear that this was not part of the plan, and most definitely constituted an emergency; everyone pulling out mobile phones to summon help. Of course, so far underground and surrounded by concrete did not bode well for phone reception.

"It must have been that blonde bitch!" someone said.

"Either way, we need to get out of here." No-one disagreed with the goth girl's assessment of the situation and, with torches on, the group piled out of the room and headed back the way that we had come. Lily and I were last to leave the room as I had to do something; get the other key from Chloe. Lily looked away as I rummaged through the dead girl's pockets, eventually locating it and slipping it inside my shoe. I do not know why I did not put it in my pocket but, for some reason, it felt safer being more hidden.

As we moved along to catch up with the others, I heard a clear 'Oh my God!' coming from the front of the line, followed by 'That's impossible!"

"What is it?" I yelled.

"The way we came in. It's blocked."

"What do you mean blocked? With what?" I asked, sure that there was some kind of mistake.

"It's been filled in. Bricked up. There's a fucking wall there now!"

Some of the women in the group had begun to cry at this point, and I could feel the panic rising within us all.

"Turn around!" someone called out. We all did so, putting Lily and myself at the front. I tried to recall what I knew of the tunnels from previous visits, but they looked a little different. Regardless of which way I thought we should go, we really only had the option of continuing along the passageway. We hurried, seven frightened adults squeezing through. *What if this is still only a show, just a really well done one?* I wondered. *Maybe I really underestimated these guys.* It was an optimistic thought, I accepted that, but it did help to keep the panic at bay for a little while longer. Long enough, in fact, for us to reach the end of the passageway. We emerged onto a concrete area with steps going both up and down. I recognized it.

"I know where we are; we can get out up there!" I pointed to the steps and shone my torch. It wasn't far to the top from here, maybe twenty steps at the most. Beyond them, we could make out another iron door, similar to the one we came in through further along the building. I rushed past Lily and up the steps, pushing against the door. It didn't budge. "Matthew!" I called down, into the darkness. "Have you got a key for this?" He came running up to where I was stood.

"I have the key for the door we came in by, try that." He handed me a key which I rammed into the lock. It went in, but would not turn.

"It's no good. Shit. Is there another way out?"

"Only the way we came in, if we can find another way around. Or we go down." Matthew did not look happy with this idea. There were seventy-eight steep steps to the bottom, which led to a wide passageway with multiple rooms. The rooms featured several lookout holes in the brick walls which had been used to watch out for the enemy during the war. It was also rumoured to be the most haunted part of the fort.

"We might be able to get someone's attention from down there," I suggested, struggling to stay positive.

"It's getting late; I can't imagine there will be anyone around. But I can't think of anything else to suggest." Matthew looked downtrodden, upset over the death of Chloe, on the verge of giving up himself. Carefully, I made my way back down to the others and explained our options, as far as I could see them, omitting the part about walking straight into the most haunted area here. No-one disagreed, unable to come up with a better plan. Then came the laughter. Not an adult's laughter, but that of a child. It echoed along the concrete walls, ricocheting towards us from where we had just been.

"Elizabeth!" Matthew gasped, his face turning grey. Time seemed to slow at that moment, as every one of us turned our gazes towards the passageway. The laughter became louder, but we saw nothing until that final second. The laughter felt as though it were surrounding us and then silence, just for a second, followed by an unmistakable apparition. A girl, Elizabeth presumably, skin burnt through to muscle and bone, holes where the eyes should have been, stood among us. We watched her mouth slowly open, wider than should be humanly possible, before she released a blood-curdling scream. It startled us all; made us all take a step backward. Unfortunately for the larger man in the group one step back meant a fall down seventy-eight concrete steps. He went with a series of thuds, falling too fast for anyone to try to help him. He must have been half-way down when we heard the crack of bone before he reached the bottom. Elizabeth was gone, all exits were blocked; we had no choice.

The stairway was wide enough for three people to stand side-by-side, so we made our way down in two rows of three, all clinging to one another with six torch beams illuminating our paths. Torchlight soon fell across the body at the bottom of the steps. I felt a little bile rise into my mouth as the cracking sound registered; it must have been his neck breaking. The man's head was looking straight at us, but his body was facing in the opposite direction. Three steps from the bottom, I turned to look back up. The torches were not bright enough to reach the top.

"What's the plan now?" asked the light switch prankster.

"If we head along here, there are some gaps in the wall. We can shout for help and just hope someone hears us."

"And if they don't?"

"Then we really need to get that door open up there, or find the one we came in by."

The six of us were huddled together as we walked, torches shining both in front and behind us. We found the first room which branched off of the tunnel; stacks of bricks lay across the floor, covered with blue tarpaulin. There were four or five holes in the wall, maybe ten inches by four. We all fought to see through them, to search for a passer-by. We yelled, we flashed our lights, but had no response.

"Three of us should stay here; the other three can go to the next room. Maybe we'll have more luck that way," Matthew said.

"We should stick together," the goth girl said, shocked by any suggestion of splitting the group up.

"What do you think?" Lily asked me.

"I think the longer we stay down here and the later it gets, the less chance there is of someone happening to pass by. But Matthew is right; it is worth checking out the other room. Don't want to miss the chance if there is someone on that side that we could have not noticed."

"But stick together, or split into two groups?" she asked, as if I was now the leader of this petrified team of reluctant ghost hunters.

"It's just the next room; you, me, and Matthew will check it out, you three keep looking out there and see if anyone comes by. We'll only be a few minutes and if it's no better we'll get back up to that door." The guy who had turned off the lights earlier seemed to see himself as my second-in-command, ordering the goth girl and the other man, who had barely spoken to anyone, to keep watch.

"Keep looking that way please; I'm about to take a piss," he announced as we left the room. The room next door was virtually identical, with the same number of gaps in the brick wall but facing a slightly different angle. We tried, once again, to shout for help, flashing our torches furiously. And once again, it was no use.

"Let's get the others and see what we can do with that door," Lily said. "It's fucking creepy down here."

"As opposed to up there, with the barbecued child?" I said, knowing that staying down here wasn't going to be an option for long.

"She's right," Matthew admitted, looking as though he would cry at any moment. As we exited the room, turning right to grab the others, I walked straight into that loud-mouthed prankster. It startled us both, but he already looked shaken, much more than he had done before needing to relieve himself.

"What?" I asked, dreading the answer.

"You need to look." His face was so full of fear that there was no denying it had to be pretty awful news, more so as he had not seemed all that shaken by the missing woman or the two deaths so far. I almost dropped my torch as I looked into the room that we were in only a few minutes earlier. I had not heard a sound coming from there, nothing to indicate what had happened. Suspended from the ceiling were the goth and the quiet man, hanging by their necks. A sheet of blue tarpaulin used on each of them to hold them in place, draining the life from them.

"What happened?" I asked.

"I don't know," he replied, looking at the ground, the walls, anywhere but at the swinging corpses. "I went for a piss over there." He pointed to a corner of the room where I could make out a wet patch. "They were still looking through those holes; I turned around, and they were...up there." His voice started to break a little, as if trauma was beginning to set in, the reality of our predicament becoming too much.

"We have to go and try the door again," Lily explained once more. "It's our only hope." I held on to her arm tightly, and noticed that the two men behind us were now also holding onto each other; fear having replaced any other inhibitions. We hesitated briefly as we passed the broken body at the foot of the steps, before starting our ascent into the darkness. *Seventy-eight*, I reminded myself, counting aloud as we went.

"One, two, three, four....."

"Thirty-seven, thirty-eight, thirty-nine, forty...." Still the torchlight only showed steps ahead.

"Seventy-six, seventy-seven, seventy-eight...." Still more steps. "We should be at the top," I said, stopping for breath. Lily's eyes widened as she shone her light behind us. I turned to see what she had noticed and couldn't process it - there was the body, neck snapped. We were standing on the sixth step up from the bottom.

"Nope," Matthew said, his hands trembling. "Not possible. Just need to keep going." And he started again at the steps, much faster than before, moving ahead of us into the darkness. We walked those steps for what felt like an eternity, losing count as we went. We could hear Matthew panting ahead of us, but always just beyond the torchlights reach.

"I'm at the top!" we heard, not too far ahead of us. Matthew had made it. We kept on until, a few steps further, the whole tunnel was illuminated. Looking up we saw them both, Matthew and Elizabeth, standing at the top of the steps. The light came from the flames which had engulfed Matthew, and before we could even speak, Elizabeth shoved him towards us. I grabbed Lily towards me, pulling her out of the way of the burning man before he reached her. Our companion was not as fast to react, the fiery, still live, bulk of our tour guide knocking him down into the abyss with a scream. Lily and I looked at each other, silently deliberating whether or not we should follow them, to see if he had survived. Maybe it was the wrong thing to do, but neither of us were brave enough to go back down there, and certainly not when we were this close to the top.

"Elizabeth," Lily called, taking me by surprise.

"What are you doing?" I asked in a whisper.

"I don't know," she replied, sounding desperate. "But I don't want to be set alight and thrown down the bloody steps, so what would you suggest?"

"Elizabeth, are you there?" Lily called out again. Silence for a moment. Then a voice.

"Mummy?" I looked at Lily, having no idea how to respond to that.

"Yes Elizabeth, it's mummy."

"Are you fucking mad?" I hissed.

"Do you know how to open that door up there, Elizabeth?" Lily asked.

"Why do you want the door open?" the voice asked. We took another step upward. There looked like only four or five more, and then the last twenty to the door.

"I thought we could play outside," Lily said, all the while looking at me. "Would you like to play outside?"

"Do you promise not to leave again?" Elizabeth asked.

"Of course. Can I come up? You won't hurt me, will you?"

"I won't hurt you mummy."

"I have a friend with me. Can he come up as well?" *Great,* I thought. *What if she says no?*

"Only if he is nice," was the response.

"He is very nice; I promise. Now, can you open the door for us?" There was a pause, followed by a creaking sound. Light poured in from the now-open door, light which emanated from the street lights on the fort's concourse. We ran toward the door, knowing that it was our only chance. I practically dragged Lily out into the cold air, running as fast as I could towards the locked gates. As we neared them, we heard banging coming from the door we had used to enter the tunnels, a muffled voice behind it, asking for help. *Blondie!* As I searched in my shoe for the key to the padlock, Lily yanked at the iron doors. They were not locked, but were stiff with age. Lily found some wood nearby, thin enough to wedge between the door and frame, providing sufficient leverage to prise it open. As the blonde fell out into the open, Elizabeth's burnt figure appeared again. What was left of her face was distorted in anger.

"Where is my mummy?" she screamed. I clicked open the padlock, yanking the chain away from the gates. I had to make a decision, and I'm not proud of it.

"Elizabeth, she's here," I shouted. The girl's eyeless stare turned to me. "Get ready to run," I told Lily, quietly. Grabbing the blonde girl, I shoved her towards Elizabeth, with a whisper of 'sorry'.

"Mummy!" the girl cried, disappearing back through the door with the woman whom I had just sacrificed. Lily looked distraught, almost disgusted by my actions, but did not pause for long. We shoved open the gates and ran, full pelt, all the way back to our house. Once we were safely inside, with every lock in place and every light turned on, we sat to get our story straight. It had to be reported, we knew that, but we also knew how crazy it would sound.

An hour after we had called the police, they arrived at our house. They threatened us with wasting police time. They had searched the whole place and there was no sign of foul play; no bodies, no Ouija board, nothing out of place. They told us that they had called the events manager of the fort and been told that nothing had been booked in for that evening - there had been no ghost hunt. The more we insisted that we were telling the truth, the more we were told we would be arrested for wasting their resources. Lily and I were stuck with the memories of that night, unable to explain them, unable to share them with anyone else. And that has been our curse ever since.

Also available from the author:

The Broken Doll
In a small town in southern England, a chance encounter triggers a catastrophic series of events from which no one will emerge unchanged. When Sebastian Briggs meets Ella she needs his help. The type of help required, however, is far from what he had expected; dragging him down a path of lust and violence. As a married father of three, Sebastian must fight between his loyalty to his family and the desire he feels for another woman, a woman full of secrets and with sinister intentions. What begins as a simple conversation between two strangers soon escalates beyond any expectations, tearing apart Sebastian's home life and leaving death in it's wake. The debut novel from Peter Blakey-Novis is a fast-paced tale, full of twists, crimes and steamy passion.

The Broken Doll: Shattered Pieces

After trying to outrun his problems, Sebastian Briggs is pulled back to his home town to confront his past, with devastating consequences. Having to deal with his estranged wife, and the unstable woman who tore his life apart, Seb discovers that he is now a wanted man; the net quickly closing in with the threat of violence around every corner. Shattered Pieces is the nail-biting follow-up to The Broken Doll, bringing the twisting tale to a shocking climax.

Embrace the Darkness and other short stories
Step into the mind of the unstable, where nightmares become reality and reality is not always what it seems. Embrace The Darkness is a collection of six terrifying tales, exploring the darker side of human nature and the blurred line between dreams and actuality.

Tunnels and other short stories
From the author of Embrace the Darkness, Tunnels takes you on six terrifying journeys full of terror and suspense. Join a group of ghost-hunters, dare to visit the Monroe house on Halloween, peek inside the marble box, and feel the fear as you meet the creatures of the night.

The Artist and other short stories

The nightmares continue in this third instalment of short horrors from P.J. Blakey-Novis. The Artist and Other Stories includes a terrifying mix of serial killers, sirens, claustrophobia, supernatural powers, and revenge, guaranteed to get your heart racing and set your nerves on edge.

Grace & Bobo: The Trip to the Future

When Grace's teacher asks her to write about the future, it's the perfect opportunity to build her own time machine! Join Grace and her pet monkey Bobo as they set off on a thrilling adventure to a strange land, and learn a valuable lesson from the creatures they meet.

Printed in Poland
by Amazon Fulfillment
Poland Sp. z o.o., Wrocław